GHOSTLY HIJINKS
AN AGNES BARTON PARANORMAL ROMANCE

BY
MADISON JOHNS

Copyright © 2014 Madison Johns
GHOSTLY HIJINKS - Madison Johns

Sign up for my mystery newsletter list on Facebook
or visit http://madisonjohns.com.

Book cover:
www.coverkicks.com

Interior layout:
www.cohesionediting.com

Contents

Chapter One 1

Chapter Two 11

Chapter Three 19

Chapter Four 29

Chapter Five 45

Chapter Six 59

Chapter Seven 77

Chapter Eight 91

Chapter Nine 101

Chapter Ten 111

Chapter Eleven 125

Chapter Twelve 135

Chapter Thirteen 149

Chapter Fourteen 165

Chapter Fifteen 179

Copyright © 2014 Madison Johns
GHOSTLY HIJINKS, Madison Johns

Disclaimer: This is a work of fiction. Any similarity to persons living or dead (unless explicitly noted) is merely coincidental.

Dedication

I dedicate this book to all of the readers who have embraced Agnes Barton and Eleanor Mason and their adventures. This series has no end in sight and with the support of my readers, there's no reason it ever needs to.

Chapter One

I stared at the stack of vacation brochures lying on the table. *I'm Agnes Barton, and while I'm a private investigator in and around East Tawas, Michigan, with my best friend Eleanor Mason, I'm so ready for a real vacation. I'm also a young seventy-two with Eleanor coming in at eighty-two. Oh, and I also have recently acquired a ghost named Caroline who has decided to attach herself to me. She's about as silent a partner as any I know of. It took some doing, but Caroline found her tongue and can speak. She has allowed Eleanor to see her, too. The jury is still out on if that's such a great idea. Eleanor just isn't used to having any competition.*

Eleanor stood there, snatching a cruise ship brochure. "This looks fun."

"With your skin, Eleanor? I think not."

Eleanor plopped herself down in a chair opposite me. "You've been at this for two weeks. Are we ever gonna go on vacation or what?"

Caroline appeared, her thirties ensemble of a green and white floral dress with petaled step heels on her feet. While she wasn't as filled out as most of us, she didn't appear nearly as transparent as you'd expect a ghost to look like. Caroline had the ability to disappear and re-appear at will, and not always when I wanted her to.

"This one looks fun," Caroline said.

Eleanor squared her shoulders, and snatched up the pamphlet. "Journey to the Old West and visit an actual ghost town," Eleanor read. "Actually, that does sound fun. I just hope there're no real ghosts there, though."

I gave this some thought and nodded. "I'm with you there, Eleanor. I've seen far too many ghosts of late." Caroline floated away, and I quickly added, "I didn't mean you, dear. I just meant that staying at the Butler Mansion has really rattled my nerves. There's always some ghost stomping on the floors or howling at all hours of the night."

"You can't blame them, really. They have to behave themselves all day long. The twilight hours are all they have," Eleanor said.

"Yes, but even then," Caroline began. "Someone is always sneaking around at night with voice recorders trying to get a reading, but luckily most of the ghosts at the mansion know enough not to give anyone any solid evidence."

I nodded in agreement. "I'm good with visiting the Old West. I've always been fond of history. It would be exciting and calm compared to here, of late. I'll have to railroad someone into watching over the mansion while we're gone. The place is booked up pretty solid."

"You could ask Martha," Eleanor said.

"I could, but only if we don't tell her where we're going. She's not likely to stay here, otherwise." I fanned myself with a brochure. Then I thought about Millicent, who is Mr. Wilson's granddaughter. Mr. Wilson is Eleanor's fiancé. "Millicent seems able-minded. Is she still in town, Eleanor?"

Eleanor's face lit up. "She sure is. I'll call her and ask if she's up to the job. We really need to find her a man."

"I'm sure she can find her own man if she has a mind to. It's not good getting too involved in someone's love life. I mean, what if we introduced her to someone and he wound up being a jerk? I don't want to be responsible for her unhappiness."

Eleanor pulled out her iPhone and called Millicent. When she finally hung up, Eleanor said, "She'd be happy to help us out, but only if we take Mr. Wilson with us on our trip. I think the poor dear needs a break from his tuna casserole."

GHOSTLY HIJINKS

Sheriff Peterson waltzed into the mansion in a hurried fashion. "There's been a bank robbery in East Tawas. I'm surprised you girls haven't been to the bank already, questioning witnesses."

So, Sheriff Peterson wants our help? Before I was able to answer Clem, Eleanor calmly informed the good sheriff that he was on his own this time. "We're going on vacation," Eleanor informed him. "We're going out West this time. Hopefully, you don't have any kin there like you had when we went to Florida, and we also won't be needing you to arrange accommodations for us. The last time you had us staying at an old folks' home."

Peterson pulled the neck of his shirt out slightly. "I believe that was a retirement village, but okay. I don't have any relatives that I know of in—where did you say you're going?"

Eleanor hid the brochure behind her back. "None of your beeswax."

"Now, Eleanor, be nice. We'll leave the particulars with Millicent Wilson. She'll be along soon since she's looking after the Butler Mansion while we're gone."

"Good enough," Peterson said on his way to the door of the mansion.

Just then Duchess, my cat, surfaced and whizzed past with the ghost dog hot on her heels. That's how it's been of late. Not only did I inherit Caroline, but any other spirit that decided to latch itself to me, or I should say, Caroline. The ghost dog was compliments of Leotyne Williams. He was her hell-hound in real life. Ever since I went to see her, that blasted ghost of her hound has been chasing Caroline … but of late, he's decided that Duchess is a better target. Leotyne was a gypsy-slash-witch that has resided in the Tawas campground for quite some time. Some might call her a fortuneteller, but her sight is subjective and full of riddles. Most times, it was downright confusing.

Millicent came through the door, a huge smile on her face. She immediately went behind the desk that sat between the drawing room and dining room. That's where guests were checked in and confidentiality agreements signed. So basically, what happens at this mansion, stays at this mansion. Whenever guests ask about the haunted history, it's merely shrugged off. Instead, they are first given the history of who built the mansion and are then taken on a tour of both the house and cemetery. The room on the third floor is off limits to guests and kept locked at all times, and not just so that the ghosts who live on that floor aren't disturbed. It's also considered unsafe, since more than one person has fallen to their death from up there. Yes, this mansion had its secrets and mysteries, but that was left to the imagination of the guests.

"Where are you headed?" Millicent asked.

"We're heading West, partner," Eleanor said.

"Anywhere in particular?"

"Austin, Nevada, to begin with, but I hope we can find an even more remote town."

"Oh, so a ghost town, then. It's—"

"We'd rather discover it for ourselves, dear. I know you're a history buff and all, but it would take all the fun out it."

"I see. Well, have fun and don't worry about the Butler Mansion. I'll take care of things just fine, and that delightful cat of yours. Will you be flying this time?"

"I'm not sure. I suppose so, since Nevada is a long way from here."

"What's in Nevada?" Andrew asked as he walked into the door. He's my beau and fiancé, but I'm not ready to tie the knot just yet.

"We're headed to a real ghost town."

"Don't you have enough ghosts around here already?" he asked with a smile.

"Ghosts. I told you so," a woman said to her husband as they headed down the stairs. "I didn't get a wink of sleep last night."

GHOSTLY HIJINKS

"He was kidding. We're going to a ghost town for vacation. It was a pun, is all."

"Oh, and the footsteps we heard last night, what does that mean?"

"It must have been one of the other guests. I assure you, this place isn't haunted."

Caroline stood next to me with crossed arms.

Anticipating her actions, I said, "Don't you dare."

"Don't we dare what?" the man asked.

"Nothing. She's a bit touched in the head, is all," Eleanor said. "Don't pay her any attention. That's why I'm taking her out of town. She really needs to get out of here for awhile."

From the looks on the faces of our guest, I could tell they didn't believe either of us.

Andrew made the travel arrangements and we were all packed and ready to go. This time when we boarded a small airplane at the Tawas airport, there was only Eleanor, Mr. Wilson, her beau, my Andrew and me. I decided to wait to call Martha during the flight so that she wouldn't tag along—not that I'd mind terribly if she had, just that it could be more of a couple's trip with just the four of us. Martha never was the type to stick close to us, anyway.

Our plane landed in Saginaw, Michigan, where we boarded another, much larger airplane that took us to Denver, Colorado, where we then boarded a smaller plane yet again, and eventually landed in Austin, Nevada. A kind gent by the name of Travis took us into town and gave us use of his vehicle when we found out that there weren't any car rental places in town.

Agnes and Eleanor enjoyed the sights through the window. Toiyabe Mountain Range was in the backdrop and Austin had many businesses along the main drag, such as motels, restaurants, gas stations and unique shops.

"Humph," Eleanor said. "This isn't a *real* ghost town."

"Oh, I know, but it still has a Western feel to it."

Caroline took that moment to float from the ceiling into the car. "Eleanor's right. There's a much better place up Highway 50."

Andrew unrolled the window. "This air conditioning must be broken. I can see my breath."

I nodded, knowing full well that it wasn't a good idea to mention to Andrew that Caroline had tagged along on our vacation. He knew I saw ghosts, but it's just not something we've ever talked about, and I can't imagine what Mr. Wilson would have to say about it. I've been denying it for quite a while now to my friends, except for Eleanor.

I flipped down the visor and stared through the mirror until I could see the back seat. Of course, I couldn't see Caroline through the mirror, but her bubbly voice said, "Not to worry. I'll leave, for now."

Eleanor giggled and Mr. Wilson asked, "What's so darn funny, Eleanor?"

"Oh, nothing. Agnes just made a face at me in the mirror, is all."

I stuck my tongue out for good measure and flipped the visor back up. I then took out the map, rustling it as I searched the nearby area. "We'll check out some ghost towns further up Highway 50."

Andrew pulled into the driveway of the Cozy Mountain Motel. We then all got out, and Andrew pulled out Mr. Wilson's rolling walker from the trunk and we made our way to the office. Outside there was a bench made with two wagon wheels that held the bench part up. Eleanor and Mr. Wilson sat there while Andrew and I checked in.

Andrew smiled at the young man behind the counter, who, by the way, closely resembled Norman Bates! He took Andrew's information and then handed keys to him. We made way to our adjoining rooms with a queen-sized bed in each.

Wilson and Eleanor went into the other bedroom and Andrew fetched the suitcases while I waltzed around until I could find a signal to surf online, searching out a real ghost town to visit and making an online reservation at a hotel that looked right up our alley.

We settled in and used the bathroom before heading back out for something to eat. We wound up at the Toiyabe Cafe and sat at a round table, staring at the menus. An older woman came over and took our order, returning shortly after with our drinks. We all ordered water with lemon and smiled, taking in the crowd. There were plenty of families and old-timers in the place.

A man came over to our table as we were talking about where we planned to go tomorrow.

"Did I hear you folks say you're looking for a real ghost town?"

"Why, yes we were. Do you know anyplace that would fit the bill?"

"Well, now, there're plenty of places you could find along Highway 50, but it's known as the loneliest road in America. It's not the sort of route you'd want to take if you didn't have a full tank of gas. It's wide open and barren, but there're some great ghost towns that way."

"How about Silver, Nevada?" I asked.

The man's eyes widened. "Why would you want to go to a place like that?"

"I found it on the map," I said. "I looked it up on my cell and there's a great hotel I booked rooms at already."

"When did you do that, Agnes?" Andrew asked.

"While you were gathering the luggage."

"Just seems like you would have mentioned it, is all. What's the name of the hotel?"

"Goldberg Hotel. It looks very western and ghost-town-like."

"I'd find another ghost town to visit," the old-timer said. "That place gives me the creeps."

Before I was able to ask what he meant, he ambled away just as our food was delivered. We dug into our burgers and fries, but I was very lost in thought about why the old-timer seemed to be steering us clear of Silver and the Goldberg Hotel. Somehow, I knew there was a history, but I suppose we'd find out soon enough what Silver had to offer.

After dinner, we caught our first view of the magnificent Nevada sunset. It was both breathtaking and colorful, with oranges, reds, and yellows that hovered on the horizon over the Toiyabe Mountain Range. I, of course, lingered outside to take in the view, and as I breathed in deeply, Caroline hovered close by. "Did you hear what that old-timer said?"

"I don't recall you being there."

"There's no sense in showing up to you and Eleanor. It would spoil your dinner. I have a sneaking suspicion that I'm not Eleanor's favorite ghost."

"I don't think Eleanor cares much for ghost's period, so don't let it bother you."

"You got that one right," Eleanor said as she waltzed from the door of our motel room. "You should have stayed behind at the mansion. We won't be investigating any crimes here, and even if we do, I'll handle the investigation. I'm Agnes's partner, not you."

Caroline made a motion like she was wiping at her face as if tears were dropping and faded away.

My hands went to my hips. "Really, Eleanor? Why do you always chase Caroline away like that? I think you hurt her feelings."

Eleanor chuckled. "Hardly ... ghosts don't have feelings. They're not human, you know."

"I don't care what you say. It's obvious that you hurt her, and now she's not here to tell me what she thought about what that old-timer said. He sure seemed to be steering us clear of Silver."

Eleanor bit a fingernail. "He said it's a ghost town. What if it's really ... you know ... haunted?"

"That shouldn't bother us. We should be used to ghosts by now."

"Speak for yourself. I wish I'd never seen a ghost—including Caroline. She really unnerves me, the way she comes and goes."

"Get used to it. She's as much my partner now as you are. Her insight into the wide world of the paranormal is very eye-opening. She'll be an asset to us in a ghost town."

"Fine, Aggie, but that doesn't mean that I have to like it," she sniveled.

I watched as Eleanor disappeared inside and Andrew made his way over to where I stood. "What happened, now?"

"Nothing, just a difference of opinion."

"I hope it doesn't have anything to do with that Caroline you keep talking about. You need to remember that Eleanor is your best friend, not Caroline. It's natural for her to feel left out when you and Caroline get together. It seems like she's more important to you all the time."

So much for not discussing Caroline with Andrew. "She's also my partner, and Eleanor has been dreadful to her. If you could see Caroline, you'd know that."

Andrew scratched his head. "Please, whatever you do, don't tell Caroline to reveal herself to me, too. It's bad enough that the two of you see her. Come inside and get some sleep. We have a full day ahead of us tomorrow."

I begrudgingly followed Andrew inside. I couldn't blame Eleanor for not warming up to Caroline. I just hoped that she didn't think she was in competition with a ghost, because that was so far from the truth. I loved Caroline and all, but Eleanor and I had been through thick and thin together. If not for her diligence, I'd never have stuck with this investigative thing. Andrew was more the sensible type, and so far he'd never actually witnessed a ghostly apparition, so it goes to figure that he wouldn't totally understand what it meant for me to see Caroline. I had to admit to myself that I was none too happy in the beginning to see her, either, but as I unraveled how she had died after being run down by her boyfriend as she was fleeing after discovering he had cheated on her, I'd grown to accept her. She's a lost soul, and unlike the way they portray ghosts on television, she was somehow unable to move on. It might have had something to do with how she had attached herself to me when I had my accident, but all I knew was that I was happy that Caroline was along for this trip. Even if we encountered ghosts in Silver, I was confident that Caroline would be able to help us out in a big way.

Chapter Two

In the morning, after we'd checked out of the hotel, we stopped at the International Cafe & Saloon, where they were promised they'd find a hearty breakfast. When Andrew pulled up to the place, it was like they'd taken a step back in time. The all-wood building had a western feel, with a false front like you'd expect to see in an Old West town. There was an old-fashioned wagon and wagon wheels aplenty decorating the front of the place, like you might have seen during the gold rush era.

We had gone inside, sitting at a table for more than a few minutes when Eleanor smiled at a waitress who bounced right over, filling our coffee cups to the rim. I was disappointed upon hearing that they had no vanilla flavored creamer. I'd had no idea that I'd be roughing it this much. It was bad enough that the motel could only pull in three channels and Eleanor heard when she complained about it at the office that NBC hasn't been pulled in since 1985! Eleanor remarked about the building to the waitress and she said, "This building was once the International Hotel in Virginia City and was dismantled board by board and reconstructed here in Austin," she explained. "The restaurant is the original saloon and cafe."

"My, that sure is interesting," I remarked. We gave her our orders and she whizzed away. I admired the wild rose bushes that we'd seen on our way over and asked the waitress about that when she came back to drop off a basket of biscuits.

"The town was named after Austin, Texas, and my mama always told me that's where all the yellow roses came from. Since it's June, the town really smells nice, but they only bloom for two weeks and then they are all thorns," she laughed.

"I love this quaint town," Eleanor said. "How come we can't just stay here to enjoy our vacation?"

"Because dear, I want to travel up Highway 50 and find a real ghost town."

"I hope you're packing plenty of provisions," a man said at the next table. "I didn't mean to intrude in your conversation, but make darn sure you have reliable transportation."

Our food was set down and the waitress smiled. Obviously, she'd overhead our conversation and added, "I'd be happy to give you folks a survival guide. You can get it stamped at the towns along Highway 50."

"I'd love that. Is it true the highway parallels where the Pony Express went through?"

"Yup. There's plenty of good sights going up the highway, but like Mac said, be darn sure you have plenty of water and provisions."

After we were stuffed to the gills, Andrew drove to a service station and found Travis, the man who had lent the car to us, but when Andrew told him where we planned to go, he told us to wait and returned with a Jeep Cherokee.

"This should do you folks much better. It's about brand new. I'll stock it with water for you. I have some provisions left over from my last trip to Silver. It's about as much a ghost town as you'll find in Nevada."

"How is the Goldberg Hotel in Silver?" I asked.

"That's about the only decent place to stay and it's still open to the public. You might want to call ahead and make reservations."

"I made them yesterday," I said. "Thanks."

Andrew and I moved our belongings from the car into the Jeep and, after buying snacks, we were off down the road with an ice chest full of ice and bottled water.

We hadn't gone very far from Austin before it was quite obvious how barren this Highway 50 truly was. We passed hills with plenty of trees on the two-lane highway.

Mr. Wilson frowned. "This isn't what I'd call a call a good vacation. I'd much rather have some luxuries."

Caroline, who was sitting between Mr. Wilson and Eleanor, giggled. "I can't say I blame him."

I gripped my purse and ignored our ghostly companion since we'd kept the 'seeing a ghost' business out of Wilson's hearing range. Mr. Wilson wouldn't even begin to understand it. His main worry was if he'd be able to find tuna fish on sale for his legendary tuna casserole.

After hours of driving in the middle of nowhere, Andrew grumbled. "How close is this town? We have less than half a tank now."

I hit the navigation system and the map had us off the road. I tapped it with my hand and it blacked out completely. Then something quite strange happened—the interior lights and headlights began to flash on and off. I held my breath as Caroline said, "They're here."

"Who's here?" I asked in a whisper.

Andrew gave me a look. "Don't you dare try to jinx this, Agnes."

"I'm not. I totally wasn't about to say that I hope—"

The Jeep came to an abrupt stop and I swallowed hard as Andrew slammed his palms on the steering wheel. "Almost new vehicle, my ass."

"Told you not to trust someone you never met," Mr. Wilson said with a pout of his thin lips.

"Wilson, this really isn't the right time."

Eleanor went into hysterics. "Nobody will find us until we're corpses!"

Caroline sat in the back shuddering. "Andrew drove into the dead zone."

"What dead zone are you talking about? I didn't see any dead zone on the map."

"Who are you talking to?" Mr. Wilson blubbered.

I didn't explain it and moved to open the door, but it wouldn't budge. "Andrew, be a dear and unlock my door."

"I can't. There's no power. Seems like we're stuck here until someone comes along."

I stared in both directions on Highway 50. "If we're not helped out, and soon, we'll be cooked in here for sure in this heat." I dug out my cell and tried to make a call, but there was no signal. "Drat. No connection, either."

"How on earth did you expect to get any connection, Agnes?" Eleanor asked. "It's a dead zone, for sure."

"We told Travis where we were going. Perhaps if we are a no-show, someone will come looking for us."

"They won't do that. Why would the hotel call Travis, anyway?"

"I don't know. I'm just trying to lighten the situation, is all."

A dark figure approached the vehicle, looked through my window and I screamed at the disembodied spirit sporting a skull for a face. "Caroline, do something," I shouted.

"I-I'm not g-going out there. He's looks real mad."

"Well, tell him we're just passing through."

"Who is she talking to and who is Caroline?" Mr. Wilson asked.

"She's a ghost that attached herself to Agnes," Eleanor said.

"Why didn't you say so? I was beginning to think she'd lost her mind."

"Well, because she didn't want me to, is why."

"I think he wants us to follow him," Caroline said. "He's pointing over to that shack on the hill."

GHOSTLY HIJINKS

"How are we gonna do that when we can't get out of the car?"

Immediately the door locks clicked and I opened the door and climbed out.

"Where on earth are you going, Agnes?" Eleanor asked.

"I'm going to follow that ghost."

Andrew shouted for me to stop, but I kept going. I had to know where I was being led. I climbed the hill that was covered with tumbleweeds and that's when I saw the building. It was a shack of some sort and I tried the door, opening it. Inside, there was a girl about five who had her hands over her face and she was crying.

"Are you okay, dear?" I asked.

Her blue eyes widened and she ran to me hugging me tightly. "I'm so glad you found me. I got lost and I-I miss my mommy."

I carefully inspected the child's face and it was sunburned. She had obviously been out in the elements for a long time. "How long have you been out here?"

"I d-don't know, but it seems like days. I'm so hungry."

I carried the child back to the Jeep, which started right up, much to my astonishment. Caroline was now hovering near the vehicle, standing next to the other spirit that faded away once we had the child buckled in next to Eleanor, who was helping the child take sips of water from one of the jugs.

Andrew stomped on the gas and we made it into Silver a half-hour later.

"Look, there's the sheriff's office. We should see if he knows who the child belongs to. I'm sure her parents are very worried."

"Do you have a name?" Eleanor asked the child.

"Rebecca. I got separated from my parents."

"Where at, exactly?"

"Somewhere out of town. They were looking for gold bars."

"Gold bars?"

"Yes. Mama and Papa said that if they found the gold that we'd be able to move into a real house."

I sighed. "Where were you staying?"

"At a hotel."

"Which hotel, dear?"

She shrugged. "Beats me."

Andrew pulled up to the building that simply had the word JAIL above the door and we waltzed into the sheriff's office that was contained in a small false-front building. When I walked inside, I saw a jail cell with a man leaning against the bars. "Hello, sweetheart," the man bellowed, and then belched.

I hid Rebecca out of sight and the sheriff raised a brow. "Can I help you, ladies?"

"I sure hope so. We found this child wandering around and wondered if a missing persons report has been filed for her."

"Not that I'm aware. What's your name, dear?"

"Rebecca. I lost my mama and papa and wandered around and around until this nice woman found me. I hid in a shack," she went on to explain.

"I'll make some calls, but I wasn't aware of any missing persons cases in the area."

A few hours later, we were still waiting to find out what the sheriff had found out. We waited outside on a bench until he came to inform us that no missing persons cases were filed anywhere nearby. "I don't know quite what to do with the child. I suppose I could call a few ladies I know to find out if they can take care of her until we locate her parents."

"Don't be silly. We'll keep her with us until you sort it out. We have reservations at the Goldberg Hotel. Check out the other hotels in town. Rebecca told us she was staying at one."

The sheriff leaned down to the child's level. "Besides the

GHOSTLY HIJINKS

Goldberg, there's aren't any. Do you remember if you were in this town before?"

"Not really."

"You might want to check the national database for missing children," I said.

The sheriff stood, "I'm Sheriff Jeff Wilford. I guess you can call me the only law in this town unless something really bad happens around here. This ghost town has about two hundred residents, many of who work at the Goldberg Hotel and the other businesses since we get tourists through the area. You might want to check out the Tumbleweed Saloon or the Willington General Store. Both of those places have been restored and reenactments are held daily at one, three, and five. I'll be in touch if I find out anything else."

We thanked the sheriff and gave him our names, assuring him that we'd care for the child. I secretly hoped that her parents would turn up, and soon. I'd hate to see her wind up at some foster home. I just couldn't allow my mind to wander back to how easy it would be for someone to become lost out there. If they were looking for gold bars, I hoped somebody knew the story behind that. Was that part of a treasure hunt of some sort? You certainly wouldn't be able to find gold bars in a mine hereabouts.

Chapter Three

We finally walked into the Goldberg Hotel and it was quite the sight inside with marble floor, antique oak furniture, and stain glass lighting, but hanging overhead was an ornate, crystal chandelier. We stopped at the counter, rang the bell for service and a woman came out of a room to greet us. "Welcome to the Goldberg Hotel. I'm Francine and I'd love to give you the grand tour after you check in."

I smiled. What great hospitality. After Andrew checked us in, we were led down a hallway. Francine opened the doors and ushered us into a large room with a stone fireplace, where two men—dressed in strange clothing, like the kind you'd expect to during the late 1800s—nodded at me. They both wore frock coats with thin ties at their collars. Each man also wore a full beard and that certainly wasn't something you'd normally expect to see, especially in the arid state of Nevada. I quickly turned and realized that Rebecca was no longer with us, and I made my way for the other room to see where she could have gone. I finally spotted her heading up the stairs and I followed in pursuit. Light streamed down the stairs and I had to nearly cover my eyes at the glare. The little girl was now at the top of the stairs, standing with a woman in a long dress that didn't look a bit like 2014 garb. It was an all-white dress and she positively glowed—literally.

By the time I had ascended the carpeted stairs, I couldn't see Rebecca at first. Carolina appeared and tried to hold me back like she could actually stop me, but I was insistent that I follow Rebecca, who at this point was being dragged by the mystery woman down the hallway. When they climbed yet another set of stairs, I quickened my pace. "Rebecca, come back here," I shouted, but the child either didn't hear me or was ignoring me completely since she didn't come back down. When I was on what I figured was the third floor, I was beyond upset. I had no idea who that woman was. All I could think was that the woman meant the child harm and she had already suffered quite an ordeal since she didn't know where her parents really were.

I strode down the hallway and I heard a door slam, the woman and child disappearing inside a room. I stared up at the oval sign with the number 109 on it and tried the door, but it wouldn't budge. I then switched tactics and began to pound the door with my fists until Rebecca finally opened the door. She didn't say anything at first, but instead smiled. "Wake up," she whispered.

I woke up with quite the start. We were still on Highway 50 and I pressed a hand against my brow.

"Are you okay?" Andrew asked.

"Yes, I think so. I just fell asleep and had the most vivid nightmare."

"What about?"

"I'd rather not talk about it, if you don't mind, but it seemed so darn real." I looked in the back seat and Eleanor and Mr. Wilson were there with Caroline, who had a sad look on her face. Since I really didn't want to start talking to her outright at the moment, I turned back around. Did I really have a dream, or was this also part of it? I had to remember Rebecca, because how could I simply invent an imaginary girl who had lost her family while they were searching for gold bars? It seemed too real to be a dream, but yet, there certainly wasn't any child in the Jeep now. Since this whole paranormal thing began for me, I couldn't help but think that someone needed my help—someone from beyond the grave, possibly.

GHOSTLY HIJINKS

Hours later, I saw the oval sign with the words "Silver" in bold silver letters atop a black sign. I figured they did that so it would be clearly visible. The entire town was made up of all wood buildings that were a staple of the Old West. We first passed Willington General Store, Tumbleweed Saloon, a bank, and the jail that I expected housed the sheriff's department. There were also a number of other businesses, but Andrew drove too quickly for me to catch the names. What were very noticeable to me were the hitching posts that stood in front of the businesses. I half expected to see outlaws racing into town on horseback to rob the bank. I had to laugh to myself with that thought. I guess I'd just watched too many westerns in my seventy-two years. There's nothing like a good John Wayne movie, and I never missed an episode of Bonanza or Gunsmoke.

Andrew parallel parked along the main street, right in front of the majestic Goldberg Hotel & Saloon. Oh, so it *was* a hotel and saloon. Before we'd barely made it a few feet from the Jeep, a man raced outside the building, the lapel of his black jacket flapping in the wind.

"Hello, folks," the older man said, who looked about sixty. "I'd be happy to park your vehicle in the parking lot out back."

"What about our luggage?" Andrew asked.

A young man pushed a luggage cart outside and Andrew promptly helped him remove the suitcases from the back and loaded it up. Andrew then handed the older gentleman his key fob and we waltzed through the swinging doors into the three-floor hotel that was yellow—or at least was once. Years of the harsh climate had taken its toll and it appeared washed out.

Clanging glasses were heard and I made eye contact with a group of young men who sat at a table that was located in the saloon. It was a small room, from the looks of it, but I'd have to check that out later. As we walked up the marble floor of the entranceway, I stared overhead at a huge crystal chandelier; the iridescent glass lit up the area and sparkled from where it was connected to the high ceiling.

Eleanor hooked her arm with mine when I began to straggle behind. "It sure is beautiful," I said.

"So far, it looks like you picked us a great place to stay, Aggie."

When we reached the counter, an older woman greeted us with a radiant smile. I almost frowned when I realized it wasn't Francine. She greeted us right away with, "Hello, folks. Do you have a reservation?"

I nodded. "I made the reservation for two rooms, under Agnes Barton."

She flipped through the book and I was able to see that the pages were nearly blank, which made me feel a little sad. From the looks of it, this was a beautiful hotel and it was a shame more people didn't come here.

An information card was handed to Andrew, who filled it out and handed it back. The woman stared at the card. "Oh, you're not Mr. Barton?"

"No, we're not married," I said. When the woman's shook her head, I added, "We're engaged, though."

Andrew's brow shot up. "Perhaps I can convince this old girl to tie the knot, and soon. She's been dragging her feet."

"Well, I'm not one to judge," the woman said.

Harsh laughter came from behind us. "That's a good one, Lois. I've known you for twenty-plus years now and why you still say you don't judge anyone, when it's obvious that you do, is beyond me."

Lois smoothed back her gray, streaked hair. "Now, Redd, that's hardly fair. It's not my fault that I'm old-fashioned. I truly don't judge anyone for living the way they choose. There's a Catholic and a Presbyterian church in town if you'd like to get married, though," she pointed out.

I swallowed hard at the mention and didn't care for a complete stranger to lecture to me about getting married. Truth was that I'd been engaged for months now, but I just wasn't quite ready to seal the deal just yet. I saw no real reason for folks my age to get married. Incidentally, Eleanor and Mr. Wilson were also engaged and I didn't see them rushing to the altar, either.

"Thanks, but are our rooms ready yet? I'd really like to freshen up."

"I meant no disrespect, truly," Lois said as she handed our room keys to us.

I took the keys and handed Eleanor one of them. "What floor are our rooms on?" I motioned to Mr. Wilson. "As you can see, one of us uses a rolling walker."

"They're on the third floor, but we have an elevator, so it shouldn't be any trouble."

"The third floor?" Redd said. "Why on tarnation did you put them up on that floor, Lois?"

She hummed to herself as she filed the card Andrew had filled out. "It's quieter up there is why. The saloon gets awfully noisy at night."

"Yes, but you know—"

Lois stomped her foot. "Darn it, Redd. I manage this hotel, not you."

He rubbed his hand over his nearly bald head. "Fine, but don't blame me if they check out in the middle of the night."

That sure got my attention. "Middle of the night?" I asked. It was then that I felt a chill rush up my back and the silhouettes of two women dressed in long dresses with bustles passed the desk. Caroline took that moment to appear and whisper in my ear, "I do believe this place is haunted."

I wanted to retort with, "Tell me something I don't know," but I kept my thoughts to myself for now.

Redd pushed the cart containing our suitcases to the elevator with a gold door that opened promptly after he pushed the large, oval 'up' button. We waited until Mr. Wilson strolled ahead of us, and once we were inside, Redd pressed the number three button. I couldn't help but notice there were also a B and M buttons. Okay, so I assumed B was for basement, but what was the M button for? The elevator doors closed and I asked Redd about the M button and he said, "Well, back in 1876, the owner had access to the mine that runs under the hotel, but it's since been closed down. They just never decided to remove the M button."

"How interesting," Eleanor said. "I sure wish it was still functional. I've never seen the inside of a mine shaft before."

"Good thing, too," I said. "That sounds very unsafe."

"Actually, there is a section of the Lemon Pine Mine that is open to the public. It's east of town."

Eleanor clapped her hands. "Great, we're so going there."

I shook my head. "I-I'm not so sure about that. I have an aversion to small spaces."

"Since when?"

"Since I've watched far too many movies about people getting trapped in mine shafts and underground caverns."

"Your friend is right. It's mighty dangerous down in the mineshafts. Even an old-timer like me can get lost in the miles of tunnels."

"I'm sure they wouldn't have it open to the public unless it was safe though, right?" Andrew asked.

"Of course, but just be sure to stay with the tour guide and not stray from the tour too far, is all I'd say. There's plenty of other things to see in town besides the old mines. They try to make most of the businesses authentic to the days of the Old West. That's why I parked your vehicle out back. Most places of interest are within walking distance."

"You forgot to give me back my key fob," Andrew said.

Redd checked his pockets and came up empty. "I sure did. Maybe I left it downstairs."

GHOSTLY HIJINKS

"Well, check it pronto, man. I don't want to be stuck in this town forever," Andrew said.

I had to agree with that one. It made me very nervous now. As it was, I had a phobia about not having my car keys in my pocket at all times. Before I could voice my opinion on that subject, the elevator doors swung open and we followed Redd up the hallway. There was a railing along the one side of the hallway and you could see all the way to the first floor. It unnerved me when I thought about how someone could die from a fall from up here, so I rushed along.

I came to an abrupt halt when I came to Room 109 and stared at the door, half expecting to see Rebecca open it, and I couldn't stop myself from knocking. I rapped lightly, but when nobody came to the door, I knocked louder.

"What on earth are you doing?" Eleanor asked as the others stared at me strangely.

"I-I…" I started.

Redd came over to me and implored me, "Please come away from that door, ma'am. That room is closed; nobody is ever booked in that room."

"Why not?"

Redd shuffled his feet. "I'd rather not say. That's why I was surprised you folks were given rooms on this floor."

"Just because one room is closed doesn't mean the whole floor should be," Eleanor said. "Unless there's a more sinister reason not to be on this floor."

Redd led the way to the next door and opened it, carrying in the suitcases that Andrew pointed out. I made my way into room 110 and Eleanor entered room 111 on the other side. I stared around the room that had a queen-sized bed with burgundy bedspread, a dresser and no television. "No television?" I muttered.

"Oh, no. Did Lois also forget to mention that the bathroom is down the hall?"

The bed squeaked as I sat on it and Andrew laughed. He joined me on the edge of the bed and proceeded to bounce up and down, making it squeak loudly as the springs made an eiee-eiee sound. I shot him a look and he winked at me, which infuriated me beyond belief. "I guess I should have looked at the website better before I booked a room."

"I know we're a little old-fashioned here in Silver, but I assure you, you'll enjoy your stay."

"I suppose Internet or cellular connection is out of the picture here, too?"

"I'm sorry about the television, but even with satellites, we've never had any luck pulling in any decent channels. We do have landlines if you need to make a call, though."

I tried to smile, I really did, but all I could think about was how we had landed smack dab in the middle of no-man's land. "Please, find that key fob. I'd at least like to feel comfortable about something here."

Andrew handed Redd a five while I sauntered over to the window, glancing down at the street below. If it weren't for the paved road, I'd have thought we were indeed transported into the past.

When I faced Andrew, they were finally all alone. "I wonder why they never installed individual bathrooms in the rooms."

"Perhaps they saw no need for it. Sure fits into the Old West theme."

"I just hope they have running water, at least."

"I'll check it out," Andrew said. "If it would make you feel better."

Andrew left, and right now, nothing made me feel better. In the distance, I saw a wrought-iron fence surrounding what I thought might be a cemetery of sorts. I flipped on the light switch to assure myself something modern existed here. Okay, so at least we had lights, and what looked to be an interesting Old West town.

GHOSTLY HIJINKS

"Your room looks just like ours," Eleanor said from the doorway. "I'm bummed about no television, though, and what's up with no bathroom?"

"It's down the hall," I said.

"That's definitely inconvenient. I sure hope I'm able to make it to the bathroom in time. I can't go an entire night without at least getting up a few times during the night," Eleanor said.

"Me, either," I agreed.

Caroline darted into the room. "This is a great place. I can't wait to meet the other spirits."

Eleanor rolled her eyes. "That's the last thing I want to hear. That this place is haunted, too."

"What did you expect, the Hyatt?" I asked.

"No, I just didn't plan to run into another haunted place so soon. I'd hoped we had left that behind us in Michigan."

"So, Caroline. You haven't met any spirits yet?"

"Oh, no. I passed a few, but they didn't stick around to chat. It might take a while before they decide to speak to me."

That's also not what I wanted to hear. "Could you check out Room 109 for me? I had the most bizarre dream while we were on the road."

"You did?" Eleanor asked. "Please share."

I paced for a few moments until Eleanor and Caroline both gave me the eye. Caroline adjusted her hat and hovered close by.

"I swear it seemed so very real, but in a way it was just too crazy. I mean, I dreamed the car clonked out and a ghost led me to a cabin where a little girl was."

"Little girl ... in ... like ... the middle of nowhere?" Eleanor asked.

"Yes. I even dreamed that we brought her into town and asked the sheriff if anyone had reported her missing. Her name was Rebecca and she was about five. The sheriff didn't have any missing persons

27

reports filed and asked me to look after the child until he figured out who she was."

"That seems odd," Eleanor said. "What happened then?"

"We came to the Goldberg Hotel and it seemed so odd. The woman at the desk was not Lois and there were a few men dressed in clothes not from 2014. Somehow, I had lost sight of Rebecca, but when I did see her again, she was led away by a few women dressed from the 1800's." I took in a few heavy breaths. "She disappeared into Room 109."

"It was just a dream, Aggie," Eleanor said.

Caroline smiled sadly. "She's right. It was probably just a dream."

Eleanor smiled. "It's about time you agreed with me, Caroline."

I was happy that for the moment they were getting along. "The thing is that Caroline told me she had gotten lost from her parents. They were looking for gold bars, and from the sounds of it, they didn't have enough money to keep a roof over their heads."

"How awful," Caroline said. "I'd go check out Room 109, but I don't want to do it alone. We should all go together."

Andrew walked back into the room, smacking Caroline with the door, but unbeknownst by him. "I found the bathroom, but there's no shower. Only a bathtub, but there's room for two," he winked.

I saw no humor in that. I had no idea how I was ever going to enjoy myself since I wouldn't be able to take a shower, at least.

"I'll meet you ladies at midnight," Caroline said before she faded away.

Chapter Four

I took a nap before dinner, and no matter how hard I tried, I just couldn't conjure up any more images of Rebecca, or what had really happened to her. I just hoped that we would find some clues to her whereabouts in Room 109.

Eleanor knocked on the door. She was wearing yellow capris with a matching shirt, her flip-flops slapping on the floor as she walked into the room. Mr. Wilson wore his customary gray work pants and shirt that made his skin look even more gray than usual. I, on the other hand, wore lavender slacks and a button-up shirt. I hooked my arm with Andrew's, who was dressed in black slacks and a tee that hugged his lean frame. His gray hair was combed back, like usual, and I always felt extremely lucky to have him in my life. He was my former boss and attorney from Saginaw, Michigan, but of course, back then he was off the market and very married. We reconnected when he'd showed up in Tawas one day and, shortly thereafter, became steady as a rock. He had been widowed for a number of years by then. I, on the other hand, had been widowed since my forties when my husband Tom died from a heart attack. He was a state trooper, and I highly suspect that's where I get my snoopy nature from. But, then again, most senior citizens had a knack for being snoopy. There's not much else someone my age can do. I sure wished I didn't see ghosts, but Caroline had proven to be a great partner.

"Are you ready to eat? Unless you're not hungry," Andrew said.

"Actually, I'm starving."

We left together, and when we came out of the elevator, we walked past a few women who I knew by now were ghosts. They simply nodded as I passed by them and the stone fireplace from my dream, but the men I had seen in my dream weren't there. I wished I didn't keep trying to sort all of this out. Perhaps it really was all just a dream.

In the dining room, white tablecloths covered the tables and each had a lit candle centered on it. Andrew held out chairs for both Eleanor and me while Mr. Wilson sat down in his with a thump. "I hope they have tuna casserole," he said. "Of course, I doubt that they'd make it as good as me."

"Nobody I know would dare eat it unless you made it, Wilson," Eleanor said.

I smiled and that was the truth. Tuna casserole was off my 'to eat' list unless it's to not make Mr. Wilson feel bad—something I'd never do.

A waitress greeted us and whizzed away with our drink orders, bringing back our bottled sodas. We ordered the barbequed ribs, baked potato, and baked beans, which was the special.

"It's going to be a loud night tonight," Mr. Wilson said. "Baked beans do it to me every time."

"I hope after dinner we can head to bed for the night. I mean, I'm really bushed after that long drive."

"I second that one," Andrew said. "I just hope that we can get a full day of sightseeing in tomorrow. I fancied myself a cowboy when I was a kid."

"Oh?"

"Yes, I wouldn't even take my cowboy boots off when I went to bed. My mother took them off when I went to sleep," he laughed.

I smiled. It was always great to learn something about Andrew that I didn't know.

GHOSTLY HIJINKS

When our food came, I must admit that we were all starving enough not to worry about how we might look as we dug into our ribs with our fingers. The dining room was empty except for us and I asked the waitress if we were the only guests at the hotel tonight.

"No, there are other guests, but none of them ever are booked on the third floor." She shuddered. "The other guests are probably somewhere in town eating dinner."

"What's wrong with the third floor?" I asked.

She leaned in and said, "I'm not supposed to talk about the third floor or the goings on in the hotel."

Eleanor laughed. "Oh, please. How bad can it be?"

"Let me just say that the last guests to stay on the third floor never made it a full night."

"You mean—" Eleanor gulped.

"Yes, they've either checked out or went missing."

"There have been missing persons cases in Silver?"

"Yes, but the sheriff always denies it. I'm sure it doesn't help that Lois's nephew is the sheriff here in town."

I drank more of my soda with a shaky hand. Was it possible that the third floor of the hotel was so haunted that folks ran off into the night? And what about—"

Before I was able to ask any more questions, the waitress added, "Room 109 isn't closed off without a good reason. Folks have died in that room."

I leaned forward. "Do tell."

"Well…" the waitress began but walked away when Lois came into the dining room.

"Figures," Eleanor said. "She was just about to spill the beans."

"Right. I just don't trust that Lois. Why would she book us in a third floor room if it was all that bad? Does she want to get rid of us that quick?"

"We're living in sin, so I can't say I blame the girl," Andrew said with a wink.

31

"Living in sin? From my recollection, you don't reside with me, Andrew. We'll get married someday."

"I'm not harping on that, Agnes. All I know is that Lois might just be punishing us since we're not married. You shouldn't have told her."

"And you expected me to lie?"

"No, but you don't need to volunteer information, either. I tell my clients that all the time, but somehow they never listen."

Okay, so Andrew was now putting me in the, *I'm not going to listen to you anyway* category. Fine, so I'll admit that I have a horrible habit of telling people things that they don't need to know, but I've never been one to keep my thoughts to myself. "I'm not your client, Andrew."

"Not yet, anyway."

I whipped a palm through my gray hair. "Ye of little faith. I promise that I have no interest in running smack into doing anything that would land me close to a jail cell."

"Good. Keep it that way."

Ice cream with a brownie and hot fudge were served last and not long afterward, I was back in our hotel room, listening for Andrew's heavy breathing that would indicate he had, indeed, gone to sleep.

Andrew had thrown an arm over me and it took over a half-hour to slip out of bed, freeing myself from his limbs. I heard a few thumps from the room on the other side and wondered if Eleanor and Caroline were up over there already.

Instead of dressing, I opted to slip out the door with my nightgown on, meeting an aggravated Eleanor in the hallway.

"It's about time, Agnes."

I pushed a finger against my lips, shushing her. "Be quiet before you wake up Andrew," I whispered.

GHOSTLY HiJiNKS

Eleanor rolled her eyes and I followed her to Room 109. I tried the doorknob and squared my shoulders when it wouldn't turn. Caroline appeared from the ceiling and slipped through the door. It then popped open and we slipped inside. I immediately hugged myself at the chill inside and I moved to switch the light switch on, but Caroline stopped me, barring my way.

"I can't see in here," I said.

"I can switch on the flashlight on my cell phone. At least that part of my phone works," Eleanor said, meaning that ever since we'd rolled out of Silver, our cell service had died.

Eleanor powered on her flashlight tool and we began to walk around the room. Cobwebs had taken over the room and they hung down from the ceiling from what we could see. From the display on Eleanor's iPhone, it was only eleven o'clock and I gazed out the window briefly. Not a soul was moving around outside.

I first walked to the dresser and began to pull out drawers and felt around the inside of them, but only came back with a thick layer of dust. I hugged myself as the chill in the room seemed to intensify, and I froze when I heard the sound of laughter coming from the far side of the room.

"Wh-what is th-that?" Eleanor asked with a shaky voice.

"You heard that, too?"

"Did you hear that too, Caroline?" I asked, but she was nowhere to be seen. "It appears that Caroline has left," I said.

"And I'm not far behind her," Eleanor said as she darted for the door.

"Come back here, you chicken heart. Don't you dare leave me alone in here."

Eleanor tried to open the door, but it only rattled. "We're locked in," she screamed.

"Shhhh. We're gonna get caught."

"As long as we get out of this room, I'm game."

"Fine, turn on the light switch, then."

Eleanor flipped the light switch on, but it only made a clicking noise. Oh, great. Now we were stuck inside and in the dark. I made my way across the room. I figured I might as well check out the bed since we were stuck in there anyway. The truth was, I heard a voice beckon me closer. "Don't be afraid," it said, while inside my head it screamed for me to stay away. My curiosity won over, and when I reached the bed, a new voice told me to run. Instead, I reached down and felt the top of the bed since the flashlight didn't offer enough light. Instead of merely encountering the dusty mattress, I felt something quite lumpy. At the head of the bed was a globed form and I jerked back when I felt the bumpy surface with hair attached to it. That's when the screaming started. I raced over to where Eleanor stood, trying with all her might to open the door. "Let me try," I said as I pushed her aside. I turned the doorknob and did a silent prayer for it to open, and when it did, I raced out, pulling Eleanor into the hallway with me and slammed the door closed behind us.

Eleanor and I had our bodies pressed against the wall with heaving bosoms until the door to my room flew open and Andrew raced into the hallway. "What on earth, Aggie?"

"Bad choice of words," I said. "W-We went to check out Room 109 and there's a corpse in there."

"No wonder that room is closed," Eleanor said, trying to remain calm. "What should we do?"

"Call down to the desk, I suspect."

Andrew escorted us into our room and I let Andrew make the call from the landline phone on the nightstand. While we waited for someone to check out Room 109, Andrew asked, "Why on earth did you girls go in that room? Redd told us that room was closed."

"I-I'm sorry. I just had to check out that room." I then filled Andrew in about my dream in detail."

"I still don't understand. Why did you go in that room?"

"Because I had hoped to find Rebecca, and I might very well have," I panted.

Andrew scratched his head. "So, let me get this straight. You actually think the remains of the little girl from your dream, Rebecca, are in Room 109?"

I nodded my head. "I know how crazy it seems, but perhaps my dream was trying to tell me something."

He sighed. "I'm not sure what to say here. Not long ago you told me you could see ghosts, and now you actually think your dreams mean something more than REM sleep?"

"It seemed so real that I just have to stop by to see the sheriff, and soon."

Eleanor sat on the bed. "And what for, exactly?"

"To see if he's the sheriff from my dream."

I stared from Andrew to Eleanor, knowing they both thought I was a brick shy of a full load. I whirled when I heard the squeaky wheels from Mr. Wilson's rolling walker behind me. "What's all the excitement about?"

I smiled. "Oh, nothing much, Mr. Wilson. Go on back to bed."

"How am I supposed to do that with all the racket going on? I don't know who's in the attic, but it seems odd that someone would be walking around up there at this hour."

I strutted over to Eleanor's room that she shared with Wilson and tiptoed into the room to see if I could hear any noise that sounded like footsteps above the ceiling. Was it Caroline up there? She sure as heck disappeared back in Room 109.

Eleanor squinted her eyes, staring at the ceiling intently, and sure enough, it sounded like someone ran across the ceiling, or above it. By this point, Eleanor had her arms practically wrapped around my neck. "Make it go away, Agnes," she said.

I elbowed Eleanor off me. "Stop, you're choking me," I said.

She pouted. "I didn't mean to, but this place is haunted for sure and you know I don't much care for ghosts."

"I wonder where Caroline went." Just then, Caroline flew through the wall, unsettling several paintings hanging there. "Really, Caroline? Where did you disappear to this time?"

"I'm afraid of the dark. Did you find anything in that room?"

Eleanor laughed. "Some partner you are. A ghost that is afraid of the dark, indeed. I told Agnes that you're not of much use."

Caroline made a motion of trying to kick Eleanor. "Not much use? I most certainly opened the door for you."

"Sure you did, and then we were trapped in there."

"Are you sure we were really locked in, Eleanor? Or were you so scared that you just thought the door was locked? It's happened before with you."

"Don't you dare start questioning me when yonder ghost was nowhere to be found."

Caroline trembled, and offered, "I swear, next time I'll stay put. Just tell me what you want me to do and it's done."

"How about going up there," Eleanor said, pointing to the ceiling. "And find out what's making that noise."

I stared at Caroline. "Seems fair to me."

Caroline bit her finger and then darted through the ceiling. Within a few minutes, she fell back down, landing on the bed with a creak of springs. She sat up and said, "Thanks, a lot. That's not a very friendly ghost up there."

I stared up at the ceiling and again heard the footsteps. "What happened? You weren't even up there for more than a few minutes."

Caroline flew off the bed, landing on her feet. "Nope, but the woman up there wasn't in the mood to talk and threw me back down here."

"A ghost?"

"Yes, who else would be up there?"

Okay, so now there's the ghost of a woman in the attic. "Did she say who she was?"

"She didn't exactly give me time to get acquainted with her."

"How old was she?"

"It's not so easy to know when someone's a ghost. It all depends on how and when they died, but the ghost looked like a big, black monster with a horrific face."

That didn't sound like any ghost that I'd seen from my dream, but at this point, I was positive that my dream meant something. If only I could figure out what.

When I heard a noise outside and led the pack out there, I faced down Lois. "What seems to be the problem up here?"

I hated to admit that I was poking around in Room 109 since it was closed and all, but how else would I be able to tell them what I found, or thought I had found? "In Room 109, I found what I think might be the remains of some poor soul."

"Why in tarnation did you do that when that room has been closed?"

"How long are we talking here? How many years?"

Her hands went to her hips. "I'm not sure how you handle yourself back home, but here in Silver we don't go poking around where we're not wanted. How did you get into that room, anyway?"

Eleanor shuffled her feet, and then said, "The door was open?"

"Yes, it was open," I winked only for Eleanor to see.

"I highly doubt that."

I arched a brow. "Oh, no?"

Lois walked into Room 109, flicking on the lights, and I followed her into the room that was just as I had experienced, but in the dark. There was a dresser and plenty of cobwebs. I led the way to the bed and, sure enough, there was a decomposed body lying in the bed under a torn sheet.

At my discovery, I swallowed back bile. The body was devoid of skin or tissue and although I was hardly an expert, I believed this body had been here for a century at least. The body was in the fetal position and it was hard to tell if it was an adult or child.

Andrew entered the room. "You'd better get the sheriff over here."

Lois didn't say a word, only nodded as she left the room. We waited back in our room, mulling over what might have happened to the victim in Room 109.

"Well," Mr. Wilson began. "The poor soul might have just died of natural causes."

"True, but since the remains were found in a closed off room, it makes me wonder how the owners of this hotel wouldn't know that a body was in here. I mean, didn't they at least check?"

"Why would they check a room if it was closed?" Eleanor asked. "Seems to me that they all but ignored the third floor."

"True, but our room was quite neat and tidy, with none of the cobwebs that you saw in Room 109. It does seem that they never went into that room, but it makes me wonder how long this hotel was owned and by whom."

Andrew pulled out a bottle of wine from his suitcase and opened it. "I was saving this bottle, but I, for one, could use a drink."

I searched for glasses, but since there were none, we took turns and drank straight from the bottle. Mr. Wilson wiped his mouth after taking a drink. "This sure is a good bottle of wine. Let me guess—1952 Port?"

When I took my drink, I about hacked it back up since it was plenty strong. "Wow," was all I could muster.

Eleanor smiled after her drink. "This is stronger than a shot of whiskey."

"If you drank too much of this, you'd start seeing double," I said with grimace, rubbing my stomach thoughtfully.

"Or more ghosts," Eleanor added.

Andrew cocked a brow. "Please, not any more mention of ghosts from either of you. Can't we enjoy our vacation without staying at a haunted hotel?"

"Sure you can, but this is a ghost town, after all."

"Meaning that it's not as populated, not that it's haunted."

I wanted to remind him that any place that dated back in time had the potential to be haunted, but seeing as how he wasn't of like mind as Eleanor and I were about the supernatural, I just smiled and said, "Yes, dear. Whatever you say, dear."

Eleanor fanned her face. "Oh, great. Quick! We need an exorcist. If Agnes is saying 'yes dear', she must be possessed."

"And why is that? Can't I simply agree with the man I love every once in a while?"

"Sure you can, but it's not like you."

Before I was in the position to say anything, there was a knock at the door. Andrew opened it and Lois was there with a young man who pulled a notepad from the pocket of his shirt, clicking his ballpoint pen open. "I'm Sheriff Bradley. Which one of you found the remains?"

Eleanor stepped forward. "Sheriff?" she asked. "You hardly look eighteen."

He rubbed the back of his short hair and smiled. "Twenty-one to be exact. Let's just say that not too many people wanted to be the sheriff in this one-horse town," he said as he clicked his tongue.

"Is that an attempt at humor, young man?" Eleanor asked with a straight face. "It's hardly the time." She then pointed at me. "Agnes found the remains."

"What a way to throw an old friend under the bus, Eleanor," I said.

"What? I was there, but you were the one who realized it was a body."

The sheriff scratched his head now with his pen. "Are you some sort of an expert on finding remains?"

"Oh, no. I must admit that I've found one on occasion, but not under circumstances quite like this. Why did you book us in rooms on the third floor when a room is closed up here?" I asked Lois.

39

"I told you already, it's quieter up here."

"Not with the sounds coming from the attic," Mr. Wilson said. "It sounds like someone is walking up there."

"Probably varmints of some sort," the sheriff said. "We have plenty of them hereabouts."

I had the sneaking suspicion that the sheriff was acting out the part of a sheriff, instead of actually being one. "How long have you been a sheriff here?"

"Two years yesterday. I assure you, I'm quite capable of handling any case that might come my way."

"Ever handle a murder investigation?" Eleanor asked.

"Well, no."

"So what type of crimes do you usually handle here in Silver?"

"I don't, really, except for the occasional drunk that needs to sleep it off."

"You should probably call someone else to handle the investigation, then," I suggested.

Lois folded her arms across her chest. "What in tarnation for? From the looks of the body, it must have been here for a century."

"Oh, and do you have any forensics background that led you to that assumption?" I grilled her.

"Well, no."

"You need to radio in for extra help," I insisted.

"Why?" the sheriff asked, showing obvious irritation by the narrowing of his eyes.

"There are procedures that must be followed. An autopsy needs to be done and possibly an anthropologist called in to determine just how old the remains are."

"The most we can do for now is to retrieve the remains and put them in cold storage. We could use the ice locker at the Maverick. It's one of the local clothing stores," he went on to explain. "At one time, it was a local diner, but the new owner converted the business to carry western apparel," he said.

GHOSTLY HIJINKS

I forced a smile on my face because I was too horrified to do anything else and I didn't want them to know what I really thought — that putting human remains into a meat locker that one time housed food seemed so … *Ewww* … to me.

Lois suggested we check out the remains and we followed the sheriff whom Eleanor was now ogling. The remains seemed even more eerie with the lights on. I reminded myself to remember to wash my hands.

Sheriff Bradley leaned down and lifted a piece of fabric. "Appears to be a dress. I think this is a woman."

"I gathered that much myself. It's so hard to tell much of anything since the body is in the fetal position," I said.

"True. I'll try to get ahold of someone on the landline in the morning."

"You talking about telephone?"

"Yeah, don't you have a computer?" Eleanor asked.

"Not with the mountains all around us. We live a simple life here."

"So, remind me again, how long has it been since anyone's been in this room?" I asked Lois.

"I've been here twenty years, and from all accounts, Room 109 has been closed up for much longer, or so the owner says."

"So what do you know about the room?"

"In particular, two people have reportedly lost their lives in that room. I suppose it must have made sense to the people who owned this hotel at one time to keep it closed up tight."

"I'm confused. I thought you said the room has been closed up for a long time?"

"Yes, but there are plenty of rumors about this hotel."

"So, how long have you been at this hotel, exactly?"

"Twenty years. Francine Pullman owns the place. She lives east of town."

That sure had me interested now, since Francine was a name I recognized from my dream. "Thanks." I didn't bother to say that would be the first place we'd be heading to ask a few questions. "Do you have any more questions for us, Sheriff?"

"Ask them how they got in this room when the door was locked." Lois said. "I don't even have a key to this room."

"I thought you weren't supposed to go into Room 109?"

"I wasn't, but I couldn't help but notice how there isn't a key to this room." I opened a closet and stared into the empty space.

"What are you doing?" Lois asked.

"I just wondered if there were any possessions left in here, is all."

"I insist that you all vacate this room, now."

"Not so hasty. I could use a hand moving the body into a body bag. If someone would like to help, that is," the sheriff said.

When Andrew nodded, the sheriff darted off, returning with a body bag. Andrew and the sheriff carefully pulled the bottom sheet off the bed and placed it and the remains into the plastic body bag, zipping it closed. Once they'd pulled it off the bed and onto the floor a large, dark stain showed on the mattress.

I bit my lip. "Oh, my. I wonder if that's blood."

Eleanor moseyed nearer to me, gripping my arm tightly as the room began to cool considerably. She motioned to a picture frame on the dresser and when I went over there, the ghostly figure of a woman smiled sadly as she adjusted the hat she wore. I wished I had my iPhone handy so I could take a picture. I decided not to tell anyone what I had seen since Andrew didn't even want to hear the mention of a ghost, or haunted hotel.

"We should get going now, if we're done being questioned," I said.

The sheriff nodded. "I sure hope you won't leave town now. I swear this isn't a reflection of how our town is. Silver has much to offer in the way of sightseeing."

GHOSTLY HIJINKS

"Don't worry, Sheriff. I don't plan to go anywhere soon."

Lois followed us to our room. "I'll send Redd up to move you to a room on the second floor."

"Not on your life. I mean, we're already settled in now. It's not your fault that remains were in Room 109 without your knowledge. I'm sure it will be figured out soon and you can go back to keeping that room locked up."

Lois smiled, and I had the suspicion that she wasn't all that convinced that I meant what I said, but she left all the same.

CHAPTER FiVE

Even after Eleanor and Mr. Wilson took their leave and I drank more of the aged port wine, sleep eluded me. All I could think about was that the poor woman I'd found the remains of had met a violent end in Room 109, and how it might be related to my dream. If it wasn't Rebecca, who could it be? Even if it wasn't related to the little girl from my dream, I couldn't let go of the idea that Rebecca was out there somewhere, lost.

When morning came, it was very dark with clouds hanging near the ground, which seemed strange to me. I took a quick bath since there was only one bathroom and everyone else would want to ready themselves for the day.

Once we finally made it downstairs, our server told us there was a dust storm brewing and to keep indoors as much as possible. Redd had met us and given Andrew back the key fob for the Jeep, apologizing for misplacing it, but since Andrew was the man he was, he told Redd it was fine.

Lois was absent, but that didn't bother me a bit since that woman rattled my cage. I just couldn't believe that Room 109 really hadn't been entered since who knows when. What I really wanted to do was pay the owner, Francine, a visit, if only to see if she was the one in my dream if for no other reason, but with a dust storm imminent, it might just not happen today.

Andrew waved a hand in front of my face. "Earth to Agnes Barton."

I then stared at him. "Would you mind horribly if I asked you to not do that?"

"Fine, but I've been trying to get your attention for ten minutes now. What's going on inside that beautiful head of yours?"

"Just trying to sort out a few things."

"I hope it's not related to the remains you found. This isn't East Tawas, with a tolerant sheriff."

"I hardly think Sheriff Peterson is tolerant."

"He's way tolerant. Otherwise you'd have been locked in a jail cell long ago for interfering with an investigation."

"The sheriff can put on airs sometimes, but he's not that bad," Eleanor said. "I think he expects our involvement on cases now. Just think how much money he's saving with the county funds."

Andrew waved the server over for more coffee. "So what would you suggest we do with a dust storm coming?"

"Stay indoors, is my suggestion. I'd be happy to fetch you a deck of cards."

"How about the saloon in the hotel? Is it worth checking out?" I asked.

"Oh, you can do that if you want, but there're some pretty ornery fellas in there. I, for one, stay far away. I'm not into reenactments, if you know what I mean."

"Reenactments?" I asked.

"Sure, most places in town do them. There's a few gals that dress up like saloon girls, even."

"Thanks for the tip, but how safe do you think it would be to head out to the owner, Francine Pullman's, house?"

"That's a few miles from town and I'd say that's not a good idea until after the storm passes. It's a more lonesome road going that way for someone that doesn't know the area." She became deadly serious now. "During a dust storm, your car could clonk out and you'd be stranded for sure. Dust storms have a way of doing that to a car. By the time someone realized you're even missing, you'd be goners for sure." She smiled then. "I'm not trying to scare you, just giving it to you straight."

"Thanks. What did you say your name was, again?"

"Name's Bonnie. It's been a real pleasure serving you folks and I'd hate for any of you to turn up missing."

I wasn't sure if it was the way she said it or what, but I had to press her. "You've said that folks have gone missing around here before? How about recently?"

Bonnie pushed back a few strands of her blonde hair and then looked over her shoulder. "I shouldn't say. Lois doesn't like us telling folks about the missing tourists."

I nodded, taking a sip of my coffee. When I set it back down, I said, "Well, I promise she'll never hear it from my lips."

Bonnie waltzed away, completing her rounds of pouring coffee for the other patrons, returning a few minutes later. "Fine, I'll tell you. A few people have disappeared, one of them a young family."

"What do you think happened to them?"

"Not sure, but they left all their belongings behind. I heard talk around town that they were looking for gold, which is why some folks come here. Everyone seems to think that they'll somehow take a tour at the Lemon Pine Mine and find a gold nugget or two, but there are limits to how far tourists are allowed to go. You could get lost pretty easily in the miles and miles of mine tunnels."

"So you're not positive where the family might have disappeared?"

"I wish I could be of more help, but sadly, no. I can't help but worry since they had a child that was only about five years old."

That rang a bell. "Was she a blonde with blue eyes?"

"Sure was. A lovely girl, at that."

This might be a coincidence, but I couldn't image that it was. I was convinced that Rebecca and her family were lost somewhere and it was my responsibility to find them before they were corpses—or I hoped, anyway.

Caroline appeared, sitting on chair near our table, observing for the moment.

"Thanks again for all your help, Bonnie. I think we'll check out the saloon," I said, loud enough for Lois to hear as she happened past the table.

After we were all stuffed, we made our way into the saloon. Several Old West men dressed in the garb of the 1800s era, complete with gun belts and revolvers, leaned against the bar, all but ignoring us.

We stood at the bar and ordered a sarsaparilla, waiting until they were handed to us before we sat down at a table. Once we were seated, I stared down a man who wore chaps, a strand of wheat clenched between his teeth. He stared right back, trying to look quite like a desperado, until he winked.

Another man shot off the barstool and made way for our table. "Howdy, strangers. What brings you to town?"

"The gold," I said.

He cocked a brow. "Well, you came to the wrong place. This town hasn't seen gold in a hundred years. Unless you're looking for fool's gold."

"Not hardly, but what about gold bars? I've heard there's a treasure lurking hereabouts. Is there any truth to that?"

The man shuffled. "I need a whiskey for sure now." He walked away and I had hope that there might indeed be treasure.

"What's up with you, Agnes? What is this about gold bars?" Andrew asked.

"I heard about it, is all. If I find that treasure, it might offer answers to what really happened to the child from my dream yesterday."

Andrew stood and said, "I think I'm ready for a stiff drink, too."

GHOSTLY HiJiNKS

I watched as Andrew went to the bar.

"Missing gold bars?" Mr. Wilson said. "If it's real, someone might have found it already."

"Or it's lost somewhere out there."

The man returned and said, "Not really sure how you heard about Leister's gold, but this much I know: whoever goes looking for that gold never finds their way home again." He walked away now, and I still had more questions, like where the gold bars were and how we'd find it.

"Stop it, Agnes," Andrew began when he returned. "This is not part of our schedule."

"I didn't know we were on a schedule. Since we're not, I recommend getting off the beaten path and really discover what makes this great state of Nevada so great."

Andrew massaged his brow now and I just knew that I'd caused him to have a headache, but I just wasn't ready to remain silent any longer. I'd just try to not mention the seeing ghost's part.

A flamboyant woman with vibrant red hair, wearing a green, saloon-style dress with a low neckline, which created an authentic Old West look, sauntered over to our table. "Hello, there handsome," she said to Andrew, who tried to not to laugh.

"Hello."

She pulled a deck of cards out of her cleavage. "How about a game of poker, fellas?"

Mr. Wilson's eyes were glued to the woman's assets. "Sounds great, sweetie."

She waved her arm toward a table in the far corner. "Well, come on over, then."

Eleanor's eyes were slits now. "Mr. Wilson, I won't have you cavorting with floozies."

It was too late. Mr. Wilson stood up and, using his walker, he rolled his way over there with a huge smile on his face. "I'd better go

49

over there and help out the old fella. For some reason, I think that gal might just take all of his money," Andrew said as he made a hasty retreat, following Wilson.

"Don't worry, Eleanor," I said. "He's just having a little fun."

"Did you see how he was staring at the woman's chest?"

"Yes, but men can't help doing that when it's out in the open like that."

A tall man in western gear waltzed his way over to our table, his spurs hitting the wood floor as he moved closer. "Hello, there, ladies. Badass Bart here, at you disposal. I reckon your menfolk ain't too smart, leaving gorgeous gals like you to your own defenses."

Eleanor smiled. "Our menfolk don't need to protect us. We're quite resourceful, you know."

"You are? Hope you don't mind if I cop a squat. It's been an exhausting journey to Silver," he said as he plopped down in a chair next to Eleanor. "What's your name, hon?" Bart asked her.

Eleanor giggled for a full minute before she gushed, "Eleanor, but my friends call me El."

"That's good, because I can see our friendship blossoming over the course of the evening." He winked.

I didn't mind a little role-playing, but I just hoped it didn't go too far. Eleanor was the type that loved the attention of men, but since I also noticed that Mr. Wilson had an eye glued over at our table, I wondered if there might be a real showdown before long.

"I think you'd better go find yourself another table to sit at, Mr. Badass. Her man is heading this way."

Sure enough, Mr. Wilson had a determined look on his face as he strutted back to our table. Up the walker rolled, Mr. Wilson strutted a few feet, and then the walker moved again. It was like watching the tortoise trying to beat the rabbit in a race.

When Mr. Wilson finally made it to our table, he pointed a bony finger at Bart. "Back away from my woman, y-you desperado. She's with me." He pointed at his thin chest.

GHOSTLY HIJINKS

Badass Bart stood and a sinister laugh echoed out. "Those are fighting words. I'll meet you out front in ten minutes for an old-fashioned gunfight."

"I'll be there," Mr. Wilson said as he shook a bony fist in the air, menacingly.

My mouth hung open now. "Gunfight?" I blurted out. "Mr. Wilson doesn't even own a gun."

The redhead appeared, dangling a gun belt from her hand, and Andrew helped Mr. Wilson put it on. Since Mr. Wilson was quite emaciated-looking as it was, a good portion of the belt had to be tucked into the back of his trousers.

"This is not a good idea," I said as Eleanor wiped at a tear from her eye. "Oh, Mr. Wilson, please don't go out there. That man looks like a real gunslinger. Whatever would I do if he kills you dead in the street?"

"Not to worry, s-sweetie. I can't allow that man to put the moves on my girl and get away with it."

I stared at Andrew, who had a huge smile on his face, and said, "Don't worry about Mr. Wilson. He'll put that man in his place right quick."

We watched the clock as it clicked out the seconds, which turned into minutes. A few minutes before the arranged gunfight time, Mr. Wilson drank a shot of whiskey and made his way for the door of the hotel.

I pleaded with Andrew, "Stop him, Andrew. He'll be killed."

"I can't do that. I tell you, he has the edge."

This was going downhill by the minute and I felt my stomach drop when Mr. Wilson went through the swinging doors. The wind was blowing and dust now covered the concrete of the street. Badass Bart was waiting for Mr. Wilson and they faced off. "Time to give up or die," Mr. Wilson said.

Eleanor clung to me, crying. "Oh, no. Please, Mr. Wilson, don't do this. Don't lay your life on the line for little ole me."

A crowd gathered and everyone just stood there. Just stood there and did nothing while Mr. Wilson and Badass Bart were back to back. They each took twenty paces, turned, and were planning to put their guns to good use and commence firing, but of course it took Mr. Wilson some time to turn since he used a walker. They both poised their hands over their guns and Mr. Wilson's hand shook quite badly. I made a move to stop this madness, but Andrew pulled me back and held me against him.

Both men made a grab for their guns and it took Mr. Wilson a few moments before he was able to pull out his pistol. The guns went off and Mr. Wilson grabbed his chest. "He got me," he yelled as he went to the ground in slow motion.

Eleanor rushed to Mr. Wilson and cradled his head in her lap. "Oh, why Lord, did you take my man from me?" she cried.

I glared at Badass Bart who was doubled over in laughter. "This was the best one yet."

"I-Is this a reenactment?" I asked Andrew, punching his arm.

He rubbed his arm and said, "Well, yeah. You didn't think I'd let Mr. Wilson have a real gunfight with a desperado, did you?"

I was so angry with them all since they all were in on the gag and had left me out of the loop. "You'd better help Wilson off the ground. I don't think he can get up by himself."

Andrew helped Mr. Wilson up and we all went back into the saloon for a stiff drink that tasted pretty much like more sarsaparilla. After we all were hunkered down in our chairs, I asked, "When did you set this up?"

"While you were in the bathroom," Andrew said. "Mr. Wilson wouldn't let me do it. He insisted he be the one to have an authentic gunfight."

"We'll give you the tape at checkout," Redd said as he joined us. "Silver is pretty well known to have a little fun. And the dust storm came at exactly the right moment, don't you think?"

GHOSTLY HIJINKS

"Yes," I agreed. "But I must admit, you all had me going and I almost had a heart attack. Please join us for a drink."

"Don't mind if I do," he said as he sat. "So I heard you found remains in Room 109."

"Yes, don't remind me. Did you have any clue there was an actual dead body in this hotel?"

He gulped down a drink when the saloon girl brought it. "Dead bodies and this hotel kinda go hand in hand. It has quite a history."

"Which I'd love to hear more about."

"Well, quite a few people have died on the third floor, and folks have heard strange noises late at night."

Caroline chose this moment to appear and nodded.

"What about in the attic? I've heard tell that some folks have heard footsteps up there."

"I image they just might have. Might just be Elizabeth. She was a prostitute that Jessup Goldberg had taken up with. He secretly gave her a room, unbeknownst to anyone. Most thought she was his niece. Well, that sure seemed mighty suspect to most folks, but they minded their own business since he was the owner, after all."

"Let me guess, in Room 109?"

"You guessed right, but after a time, she was no longer seen by anyone. Some believed that she was restrained in that room after she became pregnant. Some say you could hear her pleas."

"And they did nothing?" I asked, shocked.

"The thing is that this was in 1876, and nobody knows for sure if the stories were true or not, or just stories disgruntled workers spread after they were fired for improprieties, which were commonplace in the gold rush days. It was known that Jessup cracked down on his staff if they cut out of line."

"What a hypocrite."

"True, but with money comes privilege."

"What happened to Elizabeth and her baby?" Eleanor asked.

"That's up for dispute. Some say that she was killed by Jessup, while others say she died during childbirth."

"And the baby?" I asked.

Redd drained his glass. "They say he took it and dumped it in a mine shaft right under this hotel. There are plenty of stories from tourists that claim they can hear the sound of a baby crying in the bowels of the hotel."

I gulped and I couldn't help it when a tear escaped, trailing its way down my face. "How sad."

Redd handed me a napkin. "I should have kept that story to myself."

"No, it's fine. It just breaks my heart to know a baby would be discarded so callously," I blubbered.

"What happened to Jessup Goldberg?"

"He died of pneumonia in 1878."

"Karma," Eleanor said.

"Might just be, dear lady," Redd agreed.

"Who had the mines dug under the hotel?"

"Jessup did in hopes of finding gold. With the cost of building the hotel, he fell on hard times and the hotel closed."

"Oh, really? And during the gold rush years, too?"

"Seems like he wasn't able to pay off his loans."

"So what happened after that? Who reopened the hotel?" I asked.

"You might want to ask Francine Pullman. She's the owner of the hotel now. She knows a whole lot more about the history of this place than I do. She also might be able to tell you if the Elizabeth story is true or not."

"Seems like you know quite a bit of the history yourself."

"Folks around here talk, but I'm not originally from Silver."

"Oh, no? What's your story?"

"Don't really have one."

"Nonsense, everyone has a story," Eleanor said.

GHOSTLY HIJINKS

"Expect they might, but my life isn't all that interesting to be considered a story. I used to live in Phoenix, but I was looking for a change."

"This sure is a change from a big city," I agreed. "What business were you in?"

"I've been working at hotels as a maintenance man for twelve years. That's why Francine offered me the job here at the Goldberg, and to be honest, this place was sure in need of repairs. But these days I pitch in wherever I'm needed."

"So Francine bought the hotel from Jessup?" I asked.

"Like I said before, you'd have to ask her that question because I'm not all that sure. I just know she hired me and I've been working here since 1984. I was thirty at the time," he laughed.

"I see. And now you're how old?" Eleanor asked.

"Now, Eleanor. No need to be rude."

"I wasn't being rude. I was just wondering and doing the math. He must have begun working at a hotel at the age of eighteen and came here at age thirty, so that only makes you sixty?"

"Yup," he rubbed a hand over his head. "The harsh climate of Nevada sure has taken a toll on me and made me look way beyond my years."

"I'm sure Eleanor didn't mean that. Did you?"

Eleanor's eyes widened. "No! I was just trying to figure out how many times this hotel really exchanged hands. I also wonder why the hotel would have been opened back in 1984."

"When you meet Francine, you'll know. See, most folks do things for the money, but that's not how I see the owner. She's a remarkable woman. Be sure to head out to her ranch when the storm lets up. It will be worth your trip."

I smiled kindly. "Thanks again, Redd."

Redd smiled. "You can ask me anything. Lois has gone home for the day."

"You mean she doesn't stay here?"

"Oh, no. She's a little skittish, if you want to know. It seems she's afraid of the ghosts that lurk in the hotel."

"Ghosts, eh?" Andrew asked. "That's all you need to do—fill Agnes's head full of more ghost stories—she already leans that way as it is."

"The way I see it is that some folks are either skeptics or believers. I'm sure Agnes has a good reason to believe that ghosts are real."

"I do. Actually, one is attached to me. Her name is Caroline."

"Well, then. Hello, Caroline, wherever you are," Redd said as he glanced around as if she'd appear at any moment.

Caroline giggled with a hand over her mouth.

"Please, don't encourage her," Andrew said, obviously irritated.

"Don't pay any attention to him, Redd, but in all honesty, I had a few more questions for you."

"Shoot."

Guns were drawn, and I smiled now that I knew it was all a joke.

"Actually, I had heard about a few missing tourists. What can you tell me about that?"

"You know, sometimes folks check in and forget to check out, is all. That's what happens with the supernatural goings on around here."

"How about a family with a five-year-old child, a blonde?"

"I think I remember a family that fits that description, but from what I can recall, they were looking to strike it rich."

"Leister's gold," a tall man said from the bar. "Plenty of folks still believe in that myth."

"What is Leister's gold?" I asked Redd.

Redd rubbed his chin thoughtfully. "Well, there was a prospector, a Peyton Leister, or so the stories go. He was reputed to have found a huge amount of gold, but instead of bringing it into town he had it melted down into gold bars, which he had hidden in one of the canyons around Silver. But shoot, it might just be in some mineshaft, for all we know. You'll have to check in over at the Willington General Store after the dust storm subsides. The owner, Glenda O'Shay, has the full skinny on the story. All I'm going by are stories that make the rounds. I guess it comes with the territory since this is a ghost town and all."

"My, now that sure is interesting."

"But how did you know about the missing family, Agnes? I mean, that they had a five-year-old daughter and all? That sure seems pretty specific."

I bit my bottom lip now. How on earth could I ever try and explain that I dreamed about the girl when I don't even know for a fact if she's real or not?

"Oh, well. I-I—"

"Agnes doesn't want to get any of the other staff into trouble for telling us something they shouldn't have," Eleanor said as she batted her eyelashes.

"I see. Probably for the best, since if Lois found out she'd have a cow."

"I suspect she has had a herd by now," I said with a wink.

I turned to ask the tall man that was at the bar about Leister's gold, but he now was nowhere to be seen. Figures. Hopefully, we'd be able to get that out of Francine when we meet her, which from the looks of how the dust was blowing outside, wouldn't be today for sure.

Redd stood up and stretched. "Sure nice talking, Agnes, but I best do my rounds to make sure there isn't any dust making its way into the hotel."

I thanked Redd again and yawned. "What now? I really want to talk to Francine, but I guess it can wait until tomorrow."

Andrew had his arms folded over his chest. "At least you have some sense. I half expected you to demand we make our way there during the dust storm."

"I'm not completely crazy."

"No? Well, you sure seem hell-bent on checking out a story based on a dream, of all things. I miss the days when you were just poking into murder investigations," Andrew said.

Eleanor leaned across the table. "You do realize that Redd never did answer your question about if he had or hadn't been in Room 109 before?"

"That's right. I guess I was so interested in hearing the history of the place that I completely forgot that. Lucky for us, we can always ask him at another time. From the looks of the remains, it appears that it's been in that room for quite a spell, like before Redd was even born, for all we know."

"It's not like we'll be able to figure out just whose body that is. I'm sure the sheriff won't be supplying us with that bit of information," Eleanor said.

"No, and that's not my main concern now. I feel like Rebecca is out there somewhere and it's up to us to find her."

"If she is," Andrew began, "I'm sure she has perished from the elements by now, or will have in this dust storm."

I nodded, but I wasn't about to give up on this just yet. I didn't exactly know why I had that dream, but some of the pieces were falling into place. That is, if Francine looked anything like the woman that worked the counter of the hotel in my dream. Sure, I also knew that I also dreamed of men in 1800s clothing, but gosh darn it, this was all I had to go on.

Chapter Six

Dust storms rank right up there with the most boring reasons to be stuck indoors, ever. Most of the day, we played cards since there wasn't much else to do and went to bed early, at eight o'clock, but from the way it looked outside, it could have been midnight.

I must admit, there was something about seeing a dust storm firsthand that was unnerving. The wind blew so hard that I half expected the roof to blow away. At least with the creaks and groans of the room, any other sort of noise was drowned out.

Eleanor joined me in the bathroom. "I hafta pee. Are you done in here, yet?"

"Sure am."

Before I had a chance to leave the bathroom, Eleanor popped a squat. "Eleanor!" I gasped, racing out the door. I stood there against the door as Caroline floated up to where I was.

"Where have you been off to?"

Caroline fanned her face. "Oh, I met me a fella. He's rather nice, too."

"Are we talking an actual alive human, or spirit?"

"Spirit, of course. Most people can't see me and I think I'll keep it that way. Your man doesn't like me much."

"He's just taking time to adjust to the fact that I can see a ghost now, or I should say ghosts since I keep seeing new ones all the time."

"This hotel has many spirits," she shuttered. "I keep hearing about this ornery one, called The Cutter."

"The Cutter?" That sure didn't sound good at all.

"He hangs out in the library. It's near the main staircase. He attacks whoever enters with a butcher knife, or so crazy Mary says."

"Crazy Mary? Is that the name of the ghost in the attic?"

"That's her. Mary and Niles were once romantically involved when they were alive, but they had a little misunderstanding, and now she hangs out in the attic."

I guess it wasn't Elizabeth haunting the attic like Redd suggested. "So, your fella is Niles?"

"He's not my fella, Agnes. He's just a spirit to talk to while you're busy investigating."

"I thought you'd be more involved than you are."

"I try, but it's not like you can talk to me around anyone. Not unless you want everyone to think you're off your rocker."

Eleanor surfaced from the bathroom and I explained to Eleanor about the ghosts that haunted the hotel. She rolled her eyes. "Cutter, indeed," she said as she stomped away.

"I thought if Eleanor could see me it would be easier, but she's so stubborn, that one."

"I don't know what to say. She's really never been like this. She knows perfectly well that ghosts exist, but it seems like she's gone into denial now."

"Maybe that's her way of dealing with seeing ghosts."

"The thing is, she doesn't seem to see nearly the amount I do and I just don't understand why."

"You have a gift now and you need to come to terms with it."

"Sometimes I wish I didn't have it. I like you and all, but the other spirits are a bit unnerving at times. The big thing is this dream I had. I'm positive that I need follow up on it and find that little girl. She's lost and it's up to me to find her."

"I'm just not so sure, Agnes, but if that's what you want to do, you should do it no matter what anyone thinks."

GHOSTLY HIJINKS

Caroline faded away before I could ask her any more questions about Crazy Mary. Why was it that all these people around here in the west had titles to their names? When Andrew said my name, I knew why Caroline vanished.

"Yes, Andrew."

"I'm not sure what you said to Eleanor, but she said something about going to the library to get a book."

My eyes widened. "Oh, my. Was that some cause of concern?"

He pushed his palm through his hair. "Well yes, since she was muttering about Caroline and she'd show her that she wasn't afraid of ghosts."

I strode toward the elevator, and instead of waiting on it, I took to the stairs. By the time I was halfway down the second flight, I wished I had waited for the elevator.

When I was finally on the first floor, I had to lean on the arm rail and try to catch my breath, as I was panting like a dog that had run for miles. Getting old sure sucked when you couldn't do the things you once could.

Andrew met me and said, "Agnes Barton, are you trying to kill yourself?"

"Not exactly, but I need to stop Eleanor from going into that library."

"Whatever for? And don't you dare tell me another story about any more ghosts."

I straightened and searched for Eleanor, who was in the process of opening doors and looking inside.

I made my way over to Eleanor and scolded her. "Wh-What on earth are you doing, Eleanor?"

"Why are you panting like that, Agnes?"

"Because I took the stairs to try and catch up to you."

"Are you nuts? You're not in any shape to do that."

"I know, but I was trying to catch up to you, and—"

"Found the library," Eleanor said as she opened the door, making her way inside. "I'm going to prove to you that Caroline is filling your head with tall tales."

I followed Eleanor inside and we both were tiptoeing at this point, each of us looking around. Eleanor laughed. "I told you there's no Cutter in here."

Books flew off the shelf and a ghostly apparition of a man surfaced out of a bookshelf with a long, jagged knife in his hand. "Leave me alone. I'm trying to read!" he shouted as he shook a book in his opposite hand.

I backed up. "Well, go right ahead, then."

Eleanor now had her arms around my neck. "Run!" I screamed.

We raced for the door and a startled Andrew dodged out of the way just as the Cutter slashed at him. We narrowly escaped with our lives, or so I thought, slamming the library door closed behind us.

Lois waltzed toward us. "Really? What is all this commotion about?"

"I-I," Eleanor began.

"Th-There's a m-man," I said.

"With a knife trying to kill us," Andrew said with bated breath. "What kind of hotel are you running with crazy men running around trying to stab your guests?"

"There's no man with a knife in the library, I assure you. It's simply a wild figment of your imaginations."

"No? You go in there and check it out, then," I said as I cocked my brow.

"I'll do no such a thing. I'm busy."

Lois whirled away and Eleanor said, "She's too chicken to go in there, is my thought."

"Don't blame her there. I need to sit down," Andrew said.

He sat in a chair nearby, trying to calm himself, from the looks of it.

GHOSTLY HIJINKS

"Sorry, Andrew. I had hoped you'd be spared from seeing a ghost while we're here."

"Is that what that was? He sure is an angry one."

"Caroline called him The Cutter."

"So you already knew he was in there and you went in anyway?"

"Actually, I just tried to stop Eleanor from going in there, remember?"

"I wanted to prove to you that I'm not afraid of ghosts, is all. How was I to know there'd be a real angry spirit that would be brandishing a knife?"

I walked into the dining room and came back with coffee in Styrofoam cups. "Here, take a drink, dear," I said.

"Actually, I'd rather go to the saloon where I can get a real drink. Besides, I want to check on Mr. Wilson. He said there's a poker tournament in there today. I want to make sure he doesn't get conned out of all of his money."

We waltzed to the saloon, where Mr. Wilson sat at a table with Badass Bart and two other men who looked like serious card players, with the saloon girl dealing.

"Do you have room for one more?" Andrew asked.

"Sure do," the saloon girl said.

"Thanks, Patty," Andrew said.

"Patty?"

"Oh, yes. We chit-chatted yesterday, remember?"

I really didn't, seeing as how yesterday was a blur of playing cards. Now that I thought about it, I sort of remembered that Andrew and Patty were talking, although I didn't know her name at the time. Since I'm not the jealous type, I didn't mind it all that much.

"Can I get the key fob so I can get out to Francine Pullman's place?"

"You'll be lucky if your vehicle even starts today," Badass Bart said. "Dust storms have a way of clogging up your tailpipes."

I almost sighed, but Redd waltzed into the room, waving a piece of paper. "I drew you a map so you can find the Pullman place. I knew you'd want to head right out there today."

"But what about the Jeep? Bart said that the dust storm might have clogged up all the pipes."

"Not to worry. Before I returned the key fob, I made sure to park your vehicle in one of the barns out back. I'd hate for tourists to get stranded out here."

"Could you come with us?" I asked. "Like you said, I'd hate to get stranded since our men folk are too busy playing cards now."

"I'll have to clear it with Lois first, but I'll go ask."

Eleanor and I gave our men a peck on their cheeks and we made our way out to wait by the door until Redd strode our way. "Let's go, ladies."

"Lois must be in a better mood now."

"Not really, but since she didn't want to lose another paying patron, she agreed that it was a good idea that I accompany you ladies. Women just shouldn't be traipsing all over by themselves in unfamiliar territory."

"Is that some kind of crack?" I asked with a sly smile.

"No, ma'am. I know better than to do such a thing."

Redd led the way out to a barn, opening the door, and noticed that the Jeep had only a minimal amount of dirt on it. I hopped into the driver's seat and pushed the ignition button and out I drove. On the way out of town, all along the main drag, people were in front of businesses sweeping the sidewalks and the front of their places to remove the dirt. The street still had its fair share of dirt on it, but not deep enough to cause issues driving through it.

Once we were out of town, we were back in the wide-open spaces with the mountains in the distance. We were all quiet for some reason, until I asked, "So how well acquainted are you with Francine?"

"Well as a man can be with a woman for a boss," he chuckled. "Personally, I avoid her at all costs."

"Why is that?"

"Let's just say she's been lonely for far too many years now and I've always had the impression that she'd like to become better acquainted with me that I'd care to be."

"Is there something wrong with that?" Eleanor asked.

"I suppose not, but I like my life just the way it is, without complications."

I smiled to myself and knew a confirmed bachelor when I met one. "Have you ever been married?"

"No. I'm just not interested in getting married, or raising a family."

"Surely, you had to have some female companionship," Eleanor said.

Redd pulled at the collar of his shirt. "Can we change the subject?"

"Sure we can, or we don't have to talk about anything if you don't want to, but I was curious about something that happened in the library before we left. There was a man in there wielding a knife, and he almost stabbed us."

Redd smiled. "Oh, so you met The Cutter, did you? He's never actually harmed anyone, but he sure knows how to scare the daylights out of folks."

"That's sounds about right, but Lois acted like she didn't know what we were even talking about."

"Oh, but I reckon she never went in the library to check it out, either, now did she?"

"You got that one right," Eleanor said.

"Lois doesn't care for ghosts all that much and I think the feeling is mutual. That's why she stays close to the desk most of the time. They never go near there."

"So what's the story about The Cutter?"

"Well, I'm not all that sure. You should ask Francine—"

"Don't start that again. You have to know something."

"Fine, then. His name is Douglas. He worked at the hotel as a carpenter and he had an obsession with knives, but he was an odd one, as the story goes. He loved to read books and sure got awfully mad if he was disturbed in the library. They found out he was a wanted man and implicated in a few murders in Virginia City, but when the law showed up here looking for him, there was a shootout, and Douglas was killed right here in the library."

"A real Old West shootout in the library of the Goldberg?" I asked, astonished.

"Yes, might be why he still haunts the library. But other than scare folks out of there he's harmless. There are still bullet fragments in the woodwork of the library. Take a look sometime and you'll see."

"I-I'm not so sure I want to go back in there. I mean, it's rude to bother a spirit when he's reading."

Eleanor snickered. "Good one, Agnes."

I shot Eleanor a look via the rearview mirror, and asked Redd, "Did you ever work here when Crazy Mary was here?"

"Oh, no, but I know exactly who you're talking about. Mary worked as a housekeeper here, but I can't tell you exactly when. I've seen her when I went up to the attic once. She's a real mean spirit and scares off anyone who goes up there."

"Oh, so it isn't Elizabeth roaming up there after all?"

Redd laughed. "I guess not. What I told you yesterday was just one of the stories I've heard is all. I had completely forgotten about Crazy Mary."

"I heard she was seeing another man—Niles."

"Where are getting all your information? Not too many folks know about Niles and Mary. I don't even know the specifics, but what I do know is there was a murder-suicide on the third floor, and it must have been them, since both of their ghosts have been spotted in the hotel."

"There was a murder-suicide in the hotel, too?" I asked.

"Just because there was a horrific crime like that here," Eleanor began. "That doesn't mean that Mary and Niles haunt the hotel. I'm beginning to wonder if folks just are letting their imaginations go to extremes."

"Mr. Wilson heard footsteps above the ceiling," I said. "That has to be Mary, and Caroline—"

"Let's not talk about Caroline the friendly ghost now. You should have left her at home."

"Eleanor, Caroline has been a great help."

"How? By vanishing when something happens?"

"Wow, sounds like you two are letting a ghost get between your friendship."

"No, I'm not," I said. "Eleanor is just jealous that Caroline has attached herself to me, and she's helped out many times. I didn't ask to start seeing ghosts, you know."

"How did it begin?" Redd asked.

"I had a car accident and she just appeared to me."

"That sure is an interesting gift, but what you two need to decide is if you want to work as a team or not. Does she speak to the other spirits, too?"

"Sometimes. She told me about Mary and Niles, saying that they once dated when there were alive."

"Did she happen to say if Mary killed Niles and then herself?"

"No."

"Too bad. I'd sure like to know if the whole story about them is true. I bet it's a great story."

Eleanor nudged me through the seat and I couldn't help but wonder if she was trying to shush me up, which I did, just as a cow-shaped mailbox came into view.

"There's the driveway," Redd pointed out.

I drove up the dirt drive and stopped at a large house with a woman sweeping her wraparound porch. She stopped what she was doing when she saw the Jeep come to a stop, and smiled when she saw Redd as we got out.

Two black labs ran off the porch and began to bark something fierce. "Knock off that racket, boys," the woman said. "What's going on here, Redd?"

"Francine, this is Agnes and Eleanor. They wanted to meet you and get some history about the Goldberg Hotel."

"Is that right, now?"

I couldn't help but smile, as she was the very same woman from my dream and that gave me more hope than I had previously. Was it possible that this woman had worked the desk at the hotel? Before I started asking too many weird questions like that, I needed to ask about the ownership of the hotel.

"Come on in, ladies. Redd can chill on the porch."

She sashayed into the house and Eleanor and I followed. Inside was very western-like with a fireplace and wooden mantel above it where trophy antlers were attached. She asked us if we wanted some iced tea and was off into the other room when we nodded profusely. Francine brought back iced tea on a tray and set it down on a glass table. "Please, have a seat, ladies."

We sunk into the leather couch and it felt like heaven to me since it was so cool to my back. "I'm really a history buff," I said.

"We are," Eleanor added. "We heard that Jessup Goldberg actually had the hotel built."

"Yes, that's correct. Construction began in the winter of 1873 and was finished in 1875. There was a grand opening that even President Ulysses S. Grant attended."

"Wow, that sounds like a huge deal for Silver," I said.

"Oh, it sure was, but the success of the Goldberg was short-lived for Jessup. He died before his time, and with good reason. He spent too much time in the mine he insisted on digging under the hotel in search of gold that wound up to be a dry shaft."

"And he died in 1878, is that right?" I asked.

"Very good. I suppose Redd told you that since Lois is very tight-lipped."

I took a sip of the iced tea and nodded. "That, she is. She's a bit too stiff for my liking."

"She's obedient. I wish that were true of more people." She took a drink of her tea and asked, "So why are you really here?"

"We were interested in who might have taken possession of the Goldberg after Mr. Goldberg died."

Francine pulled an imaginary string from her pants. "Fine, I'll play along. It was closed down when he died. There was quite a debt and the State of Nevada took possession of the Goldberg then. It was finally sold to Ervin Hastings in 1898."

"It was empty for twenty years?"

"Yes, and Ervin spent quite a sum to remodel the hotel. It reopened in 1900, but misfortune struck—a fire that partially damaged the interior of the first floor. Luckily, the fire was put out before it spread, but Ervin was out of funds and was deep in debt by 1910. The hotel once again was closed until my great-grandfather, Wilfred, bought the hotel in 1920. He spent the majority of his life trying to renovate the old place, but he was quite a drinker and it was never finished. By 1930, the gold had all but disappeared, with fewer than a thousand people living here. My father, Barry, inherited the Goldberg in 1940 when Wilfred died of liver disease, and held onto the property since he loved the area, hoping to one day re-open it to its original splendor. It never happened and the property was passed on to me in 1983. My father was into banking for most of his life and had invested wisely, leaving me quite a sum. I promised him on his deathbed to re-open the Goldberg, which I did in late 1984, with Redd's help."

"How did you happen to meet Redd? He told us he was working in Phoenix when you hired him."

"You gals sure want to wiggle every detail out of me." She sighed. "What can I say? I stayed at West Ridge Lodge. It's near the desert, not much of a place at all, but my bathroom sprung a leak and Redd came up right away to fix it. I was impressed with his promptness and work ethic since he refused to have a drink in the bar later with me. I must admit that I was attracted to him, so I offered him a job. We're about the same age, but when he came to Silver, he was all about business. He has proven himself to me through the years with his delegation abilities as the renovations and repairs were made."

"So why didn't you have bathrooms installed in the rooms—would it have hurt to have showers installed, at least?"

"I think it's much more appealing without it. You must admit that the Goldberg sure has an Old West appeal. I even added the saloon to enhance the hotel even more. You might think Silver is just some ghost town on lonely Highway 50, but the Goldberg has a steady stream of tourists and we even have a gold rush festival every year. If you stick around, you'll be able to witness it firsthand. It's in a few days. It's the one time each year that we allow tourists to tour the Lemon Pine Mine a bit further than the tours normally allow."

I tried to absorb the history of the Goldberg, which was quite lengthy. "It almost seems like the Goldberg is cursed or something."

"Agnes," Eleanor scolded me. "That's a bit harsh."

"That's okay. I'm really used to it since malevolent spirits inhabit the place."

I nodded, glad the conversation finally got around to the spirits, one of which wielded a knife in the library. "We've experienced a few of those, but what I'd like to know about the most is Room 109."

Francine leaned back in her chair. "What can I say that you don't already know via Redd?"

"Since I found remains in Room 109, I'd like to know if you were aware of its existence."

GHOSTLY HIJINKS

"All I can say about it is that my great-grandfather, Wilfred, gave my father instructions to never go into Room 109, or even open the door a crack, but it seems that since you two took it upon yourselves to go in there, who knows what else you have unleashed?"

"We found remains in that room, is all. Some poor soul died up there, unknown to anyone for who knows how long."

"If my great-grandfather told his only son not to go in there, he must have had a darn good reason."

"Perhaps like concealing a body?"

"I'm sure you're blowing this all out of proportion. For all we know, that body has been up there since 1876."

"Why that year and not another?"

"It's common knowledge in Silver about the story of Elizabeth and her arrangement with Jessup Goldberg."

"Arrangement?"

"Yes. She was a prostitute, of course, and when he grew weary of her, she committed suicide in Room 109. I'm sure Redd told you as much already."

"Not exactly. He told us how some suggested that Elizabeth was pregnant and Jessup had her locked up in that room. That she had given birth to his child and it was dumped in the mine shafts under the hotel."

"The problem with that account is that it's off base. Great-grandpa told me that Elizabeth had committed suicide."

"He personally told you that? There's no way he could have. He died before you were even born."

"I might have seen it in a dream, then. Dreams can be so telling at times. Sometimes when you wake up, you're never even aware if you were dreaming or not. Until you wake up."

I stared at Francine. "Oh, I know. I had a dream about you on my way to Silver."

Francine laughed. "Oh, and what was I doing in your dream? Something exciting, I hope."

"You were working the counter at the Goldberg."

"That makes sense since I do that at times."

"Recently?"

"Sure, earlier this week when Lois was ill. She has asthma, you know."

"That must be why she left the hotel right before the dust storm."

"Do you have a point here?"

I drank my tea and set the glass on my knee to still it from moving since people had a wont to think I was nervous when it simply was a habit of mine. "What I'm most concerned about is a missing family. A family with a five-year-old daughter named Rebecca."

"Oh, yes. They left in the middle of the night," Lois said. "I imagine they were spooked by the bumps that sure go on in the night at the hotel. I don't think those spirits ever rest."

"Did they pay their bill, at least?"

"Not at all, which really bothers me since they seemed like good people. What a cute child, too."

"So you admit that you worked the counter when the family went missing?"

"I was there the day they checked it, but that's about it. I was quite upset when they ran off without paying their bill."

"And you didn't find that a bit strange?"

"Not really. They looked quite down on their luck. I heard they were planning to go to the mine until they found out the tour was quite limited to only two hundred feet of the mine shaft."

"Are you sure they didn't go there anyway?"

"Not really, but I suppose I could make a few calls."

"I'd appreciate it. You see, I had a strange dream that the child was separated from her family and needs my help."

"That's strange, unless you already knew the family and came to town to check on them."

"No. I've never met them, and I have only seen Rebecca in my dream. She disappeared into Room 109. A woman dressed in 1800s clothing pulled her into the room, and when I knocked on the door, Rebecca answered it."

"And that means what, exactly?"

"That the child is lost and needs my help."

"I see, but as you said it was only a dream and, as such, you should probably just forget all about it."

"Did you know her family was looking for gold?"

"I just said as much when I told you they wanted to go deeper into the mine."

"Please, make your call and have someone check out the mine. The family might be lost down there."

Francine shook her head, but made her call asking whoever was on the other end to check out the mine for a family that might be lost.

"Thanks," I said when she had hung up. "Could I ask you a few more questions?"

"Shoot, since I won't get any peace unless you two are satisfied."

"It's about the spirits at the hotel."

"Which ones? There are quite a few."

"I'd sure like a list, if you don't mind."

Francine shook her head, all the while keeping a pleasant smile on her face. "Well, there's Douglas. He's a real nasty one. He likes to chase folks out of the library with a butcher knife. He lost his life right there, you know."

"Yes, Redd told us. Unfortunately, we met him already. Not a pleasant fellow at all."

"Other than his death, I don't know all that much about him, but if you poke around Silver you might just find someone that knows more than me."

I didn't want to tell her what we already knew. I wanted her to tell us to see if what Redd told us matched what Francine might have to say. "Any others?"

"Well, there's Crazy Mary and Niles. I don't really know their full story, just that they used to see each other and parted ways."

"So you're the owner and you don't know that Crazy Mary killed Niles and then herself?" I said. "I can't image you wouldn't know all about it since your family has owned the hotel for quite a time."

"I've heard talk is all I can say. My family sure hasn't passed down rumors like that. I imagine that someone might know the particulars, but I can't tell you for certain."

"You're denying that they died in the hotel?"

"I can't say for certain. Anything is possible since they've lingered in the hotel all these years, but other than Crazy Mary stomping around in the attic, neither of them bothers anyone."

"No? Then what spirits could drive a young family out of the hotel in the dead of night?"

"Sorry, I really couldn't say since neither of us could ever know why that family made their retreat."

"Did they also take all of their belongings with them?" I pressed.

"No, they didn't, and I'll admit that did seem strange at the time."

"Did you call the sheriff or anyone else about the matter?"

"No. At first, I figured that they'd be back. When that didn't happen, it did cause me some concern, but I didn't think that was reason enough to contact the sheriff. I mean, they might have just turned up the next day and I'd have looked mighty foolish, wouldn't I?"

"I don't see the harm in that at all. The sheriff certainly needs to be alerted and I'll do that myself today," I said as I set my empty glass down and moved toward the door.

"I don't see the sense in doing that. Why bother the sheriff with such a story when it's not your place to say so?"

I turned. "Oh, so you'll alert the sheriff yourself?"

"I suppose I could. Go on back to the hotel and I'll handle it."

There was no way I was going to trust that Francine would really contact the sheriff, but thought perhaps I should give her the benefit of the doubt. After all, I was a newcomer in town. I'd sure like to grill the sheriff about the sheriff I saw in my dream. It certainly wasn't Sheriff Bradley. From the looks of that sheriff, he was very green behind the ears. Was there a Sheriff Jeff Wilford in the past?

"What can you tell us about Leister's Gold?"

"Nothing, never heard about it before," Francine said. She stood and gathered the empty glasses and stacked them back on the tray. "Good day to you, Agnes and Eleanor," she said as she walked away.

I knew I had struck some kind of a chord, but there was just no way I could know for certain. I just didn't believe that Francine didn't know about Leister's Gold, but we would be poking around in town and I had to believe that someone knew something about it.

Chapter Seven

Redd got up from the bench when we walked outside, trying to block the sun from his eyes. He walked back to the Jeep without saying a word. Once I had the vehicle turned and headed back down the dusty road, he said, "You can just drop me off at the hotel before you take a tour of the town."

When we drove back into town, I dropped Redd off and Eleanor gripped her big purse in her hands. "Should we ask Andrew and Mr. Wilson if they want to tag along?"

"No. We'll never get anywhere with Andrew breathing down our necks. Besides, he doesn't much care about me talking about ghosts or getting involved in this case."

"When you say 'case', you must mean the missing girl and her family, right?"

"Exactly. You should know that there's no way we'll ever be able to weasel out any information about the remains we found. I bet it will take them some time to process the body and date the bones."

"True, but we're going to question the sheriff, right? Or are you actually expecting Francine to report about the missing family to the sheriff?"

"She claims that she plans to do that today and perhaps we'll give her some time to do just that. I had planned on heading over to the Willington General Store and speaking with Glenda O'Shay today. Remember, Redd told us she would know about Leister's Gold."

"Francine didn't exactly say that she'd tell the sheriff that today for sure, Agnes, but you're right, we should give her the opportunity to do the right thing. I still can't believe that she hadn't already done that."

I whirled into the back of Willington General Store and surprised a few men who were in the back, smoking. I waved at them and locked the Jeep. I hadn't made it but a few feet before I noticed that the engine was still running. I went back, opened the Jeep door again, and pushed the button to shut if off.

"I really hate this keyless ignition," I muttered to Eleanor after I once again locked the doors. "I can see someone leaving the engine running and not even paying enough attention to notice it."

Eleanor nodded at the cowboys, who tipped their hats as we passed. I suppose I could have parked in the front, but I wanted to do my part to keep this town looking as ghost town authentic as I could.

When we walked on the board sidewalk, I actually enjoyed the sound of the clapboards under my feet as I walked into the Willington General Store. The bell rang over the door and a woman glanced up from her book, saying, "Well, hello there."

I smiled at the middle-aged woman with her dark hair pulled up under a gingham headband that matched her blue dress. She had wrinkles aplenty on her face and I thought this harsh climate sure seemed to age the population—at least in this town.

"I don't suppose you might be Glenda?"

"I might be. It all depends on if you're here as a friend or foe," she laughed.

"We're here on vacation, and heard that you know a bit of the history of Silver that you might share with us."

"And who might you be?"

"I'm Agnes Barton and this is Eleanor Mason," I said as I thumbed in her direction. "Redd sent us here."

She rounded the counter, her hands on her wide hips. "Why

didn't you say so before? Any friend of Redd's is a friend of mine. He's sure a handsome fella, don't you think?" she gushed.

"I can't say one way or the other since I have a fiancé. He doesn't care all that much when I show other men attention," I said, not wanting the woman to think I had my eye on Redd, too. It seems strange to me that so many people would be attracted to the man, but I supposed the pickings were mighty slim in this town.

"That's good to hear. I sure don't need any more competition in this town. Bertha Anne has her eye on him already."

I smiled. "Bertha Anne? I don't think I have met her yet."

"She's a saloon girl over at the Tumbleweed Saloon and a might younger, I might add."

"Does Redd spend time over there?"

"Yes, like most men in town when they're not working. I've tried for years to get close to Redd, too, but he's a hard man to pin down."

For some reason, my mind drifted to a vision where Glenda lassoed Redd and dragged him back to her shop. "I can see that already. I still can't believe he's still single and hasn't ever been married."

"I know, but I'm gonna win that man over if it's the last thing that I do," she said with a nod.

"That's not why we're really here," Eleanor cut in. "We heard you know more about this town than anyone."

"I can't say I do or don't, but I aim to help. What can I help you folks with, now?"

"How long have you been living in Silver?"

"All of my life. My family was one of the earliest residents. In 1850, after prospectors first found gold, Silver was founded, with only a saloon and general store built. It wasn't long before the word got out and folks flocked to Silver. Of course, the businesses weren't more than shacks in those days, but my ancestors went on to enlarge the building into what is now the Willington General Store. The

Tumbleweed Saloon was also the first saloon, although on a much smaller scale. The rest of the town consisted of tents that housed the miners who flocked to town when they heard gold had been discovered here. By 1873, additional businesses were built, along with the construction of the Goldberg Hotel. Of course, that didn't last as good as most businesses did. Did you know that the property the Goldberg Hotel was built on was once the Winfield Hotel? It was burned to the ground in a fire, and let me just say that not all of the bodies were recovered before the Goldberg was built over it. I personally feel that the soil is cursed since the Goldberg has always had such rotten luck, and now I heard they found remains in their legendary Room 109."

"So the Goldberg Hotel was built over the remnants of the Winfield Hotel?"

"And they never found all the bodies before they built the new hotel right over it?" Eleanor asked.

"Yup. You're both right. It's no wonder that so many spirits inhabit that building."

Caroline appeared in the store, but lingered in the corner, listening.

"What a horrible tragedy. How many people died in the fire?"

"Over fifty souls perished that day. It was the day after the Gold Rush Festival ended, and most of the people staying at the hotel were celebrating long into the night. Nobody's sure how the fire started, but the miners were blamed as there was a dispute over pay that was going on at the time for those working in the mines."

"That's just so awful, but I can't imagine that the miners would want to set the fire since they'd be the first ones blamed," I said.

"I agree with you, Agnes, but those were strange times since the miners really were disgruntled."

"Why haven't I ever heard about this before?"

"Oh, have you ever even heard of Silver before, or did you hear about it from your travel agent?"

"Actually, I found it online and it seemed like a quaint ghost town and worth our time coming here. I just had no idea how strange it would be, or just where it would take us."

"That's odd. I guess I didn't even know that this town was even advertised on the internet."

"I'm surprised that you even know what the internet is," I said with a sly smile.

Glenda's hands went to her hips. "I'm not totally in the stone ages, you know. Is there anything else that you'd like to tell me — about the Goldberg, that is?"

"Actually, I was the one who found the remains at the Goldberg," I said.

"How exciting. Can you tell me what the condition the body was in?"

"Not exactly sure what you mean by that, but what I will say is that it must have been there for at least a century."

"Thanks for sharing."

"Is it possible to talk about Leister's Gold now?" Eleanor asked, giving me a 'what' face when I glared at her.

"Oh, is that what this all about?"

"Actually, there's a family that might be lost out there somewhere."

"One with a child of five," Eleanor added.

"I'm not sure, but I have a vague memory of such a family."

"And the history of Leister's Gold is?"

"Peyton Leister was about as greedy a man as any of the men that came to Silver looking to strike it rich, but he certainly was also a braggart. He wanted everyone in town to know how much gold he found, which was quite an amount, but there were those in town who outright didn't like the man. Nobody in town would allow Leister to turn in his gold. They wanted to keep it quiet about how much gold the man had found. I suppose hoping that they'd strike it rich."

"Or planning to steal his gold," Eleanor said.

"Yes, that's exactly what they tried. One night, while Peyton was in town, a few of the men he worked with betrayed him and they raided his cabin, looking for the gold."

"So they robbed him?" I asked.

"Oh, no. Peyton was much smarter than folks gave him credit for. When nobody would buy his gold, he hid it in an undisclosed location."

"I can't say I blame him."

"Was he angry?" Eleanor asked, while Caroline was all ears, standing next to her, absorbing the story.

"You betcha he was. After that happened, Peyton disappeared for days. Nobody had a clue where he went, but when he came back from parts unknown, he was empty-handed. Minus his gold."

"Did he hide it or—"

Glenda's eyes narrowed. "They say that Peyton melted his gold down and cast it into gold bars, gold that he had hidden somewhere around Silver."

"What did Peyton do after that?" I asked.

"All of Peyton's belongings were packed up and he was never seen again, but they found his wagon days later in a deserted location. Since his wagon wheel was broken, folks figured that he'd become lost and perished in the harsh climate."

"But do you know for a fact if there is any truth to the story that he melted down the gold and made it into gold bars?"

"I can't say that for a fact, since I wasn't even born way back then, but the story is that the gold is out there somewhere and it's up to someone to find it if they're so inclined."

"And nobody has ever found the gold?"

"Nope, but there have been plenty of folks through the years that sure have tried. Some, I reckon, met a tragic end since they were never heard from or seen again."

That would be the truth if someone didn't know that area. "I'm concerned about a family and their five-year-old daughter," I said. "If they're on some kind of wild goose chase looking for the gold bars, it might spell trouble for them."

Glenda waltzed over to a roll of fabric, massaging it between her fingers. "Legends are just that. Nobody knows what would cause anyone to chase after a legend without thinking about how perilous a journey that would be." She disappeared into the back and returned minutes later, handing me a map. "Here's a map of the town and it might be in your best interest to go into each business to ask additional questions. To be honest, nobody has shown any interest in the missing family before, so why now?"

"I won't be able to rest until this mystery is solved, and hopefully, I can find someone who might know where the family was heading. I'm afraid that if they're still alive, they are on borrowed time."

"Peyton was banned from town for the most part, with very few friends. There's just no telling if someone knows for certain where the gold is, or who might be searching for it."

I thanked Glenda for her help and we took our leave, promising to return under more pleasant circumstances next time.

Caroline hovered on the clapboard sidewalk, holding onto her 1930s-style hat like it could actually blow away. "What a great story," Caroline said.

"Story is right," Eleanor said. "What do you make of it Caroline?"

She frowned. "Well, I'm just not sure. This Peyton fella sure seemed to go to extraordinary lengths to hide his gold. Why not just pack it up and sell it in another town?"

"Good point, but if we're to assume that the story is true, I can't help but wonder if he really did attempt to take the gold with him and he was found out, possibly robbed and then murdered," I suggested.

"There might not be any truth to the story at all," Eleanor said. "Just a good story to tell tourists."

"I'd hope they wouldn't willfully lead tourists astray, Eleanor. If they did, they very well may have endangered the lives of that family."

"I'm sure they were told that it was simply a legend."

"I guess we'll never know unless we find that family."

"Find the family?" Eleanor asked. "For all we know, they don't exist. No offense Agnes, but you had a dream, is all."

My hands went to my hips. "Then how do you explain that Francine was in my dream, and that there's a real family with a five-year-old girl missing?"

"I-I'm not sure, but you don't even know what that family even looks like. Think logically here for a minute. We just had a significant dust storm and the temperatures are in the nineties here. How would any family be able to survive under those conditions?"

I bit my lower lip, knowing that Eleanor was right, but I wasn't so willing to let this go just yet. Not until I paid a visit to the sheriff to find out if there was really a Sheriff Wilford. I didn't want to tell Eleanor that in my dream, there were men dressed in clothing of the 1800s. If she knew that, she'd insist that I just accept the fact that I had a dream and that's it.

"I just don't know, but I'm not ready to give up just yet. I can't help how I feel. I just know I have to find this family and if you don't want to help me, then go back to the hotel and hang out with the men," I said as I walked up the sidewalk, a tear in my eye.

"Would you wait up, Agnes? I didn't say I wouldn't help you. I guess I've just never been on a case like this before. That's what this is, right—a case to you?"

I turned and wiped at my tears. "It's not. I just have to find this family, is all, before it's too late for any of them."

Eleanor gave me a hug. "Don't worry so, old girl. I'm right here to support you and I'll do whatever is necessary to see this through."

Caroline smiled. "I should get back to check on the menfolk. I'd hate to leave them alone too long in a haunted hotel."

After Caroline faded away, we made our way into the Tumbleweed Saloon, which was much larger than I'd thought. There were plenty of tables in the joint, with a long, mahogany bar that looked a bit rough, but still had quite the shine.

There were cowboys strategically placed, playing cards in the far corner, and I wondered if they were planning to have a reenactment of some sort. When the table was knocked over and someone yelled, "Cheater!" I knew it had to be.

Next, a man raced over to them. His white ruffled shirt had a white apron tied over it. "Please, not in the saloon. Take this fight outside."

Fists were thrown and a cowboy was knocked into the man who dodged out of the way, watching the melee from the bar with a saloon girl clinging to his arm. One man went crashing into a table, and as the men drew their guns, the sheriff burst into the saloon with a rifle against his shoulder. "Stop it, all of you, or you'll be dead where you stand."

The fighting stopped, and the men moved to right the tables and sat down again. I didn't know who this man was, but he most certainly wasn't Sheriff Bradley. I wasn't able to see the man clearly just yet, but when he lowered his rifle and apologized to us for the ruckus, my eyes widened in recognition. "What's your name, Sheriff?" I asked.

His hazel eyes softened. "Sheriff Wilford at your service."

"I thought Sheriff Bradley was the sheriff in Silver," Eleanor said in a high-pitched voice. "One of you is an impostor."

He laughed. "You're right there, my fine lady. I can see not many people get one by you."

Eleanor gushed, "You got that right, mister. I figure you for an actor and this whole scene was a reenactment, right?"

"That's right, although I don't think I've ever been called an actor before, but we try to put on a good show for tourists. This is our slow time, but in a few days, the town will be plenty busy with the Gold Rush Festival. I sure hope that you ladies will be sticking around for that."

"Oh, yes," I said. "Can you have coffee with us? We'd sure like to chat with a real reenactment actor."

"Coffee? I don't think the Tumbleweed Saloon sells coffee."

"He's joking," the saloon girl said as she showed us to a table near the window. "I'm Bertha Anne and I could even make you a latte if you'd like. Just don't tell the boss man." She winked.

"I'd love that if you have anything in vanilla. I haven't had any vanilla creamer since I came west for vacation."

"Not to worry. I'll fix you up. I brought back some goodies from Reno on my last trip."

She sashayed away, her blue saloon-girl's skirt swaying. "Is that the same girl Redd is sweet on?" Eleanor asked me.

"More the other way around," the sheriff said. "The pickings in this town are mighty scarce."

"So, what's your story?" I asked him.

"I came to Silver for a job as a mock sheriff after my acting gigs in Hollywood came up drier than the mineshafts in Silver," he laughed. "It's fun, though. There's nothing like pretending to be someone you're not."

"I know just what you mean," I said. "Do you ever hang out at the jailhouse?"

"Sure do. The sheriff doesn't seem to mind me tending shop when he's out and about. I'm really good at taking messages."

"Is it really true that the sheriff doesn't have a computer?"

"Sure is, and that took some getting used to, but I learned to use a landline like nobody's business."

Eleanor laughed until she snorted. "That's a good one. I still have a landline back home."

GHOSTLY HIJINKS

"Where do you ladies call home?"

"Tawas, Michigan," I said. "For Eleanor, that is. I live in Tadium, a small town near Tawas."

"How quaint sounding. I'm from Texas, originally. I had hoped to break into acting, but unfortunately, I wasn't able to land any roles except for a few commercials for STDs," he grimaced.

"I've seen those ads," I laughed. "How interesting."

"Not so interesting when my mother saw them one night. I spent an entire weekend telling her that I don't have genital herpes."

"Wow, is all I can say."

The coffee was brought and frothy enough to know it was a latte, all right. "Thank you so much."

"Not a problem. Did I hear you folks are staying at the Goldberg Hotel?"

"Sure are," Eleanor grinned.

"Then I suppose you've met Redd?" Before anyone had a chance to answer, Bertha Anne added, "Isn't he dreamy?"

I stared at her for wrinkles of any sort, but she didn't have one. "Isn't he sort of old for you?"

She frowned. "You sound just like my mother. I can't help it if the man makes me feel all giddy inside."

"I see." I smiled kindly and changed the subject. "Lois sure isn't very neighborly."

"I know she can be cranky at times, but she's not as bad as she seems. I think she likes to scare folks off so they don't try to poke around at the Goldberg too much, but I'm sure you already know that. I heard you found remains in the legendary Room 109."

"Word travels fast."

"I'm surprised that anyone would dare go in *that room*," the sheriff said.

"I'm not all that sure I believe that nobody has gone in that room since 1878."

"Is that what Lois said?" Bertha Anne asked.

"Not in so many words, but the owner, Francine, sure told us that her great-grandfather told her father not to ever go in that room."

"Sounds like a plan," the sheriff said. "I still can't believe they are even able to book rooms in that creepy hotel. Too many spirits for my taste."

I so knew what he meant, but instead, I asked, "So have you had any ghostly experiences at the Goldberg?"

"Well, it seems that a few of the townsfolk thought it would be funny to have me go into the library. Gave me some story about how they forgot to get a book they left behind. Anyway, I encountered a nasty ghost that almost stabbed me with a jagged blade. Let me just say that I ran so fast out of the library that I didn't stop until I was safely at home. I've yet to ever go back to that hotel."

Eleanor was having a fit of giggles, but I apologized, saying, "I don't blame you since we encountered that same spirit. Believe me, Eleanor wasn't laughing then—she was screaming."

"S-Sorry. It just sounds more funny when it happens to someone else," Eleanor said.

"I bet, but how about we don't talk about that creepy hotel anymore," the sheriff said.

I was happy to change the subject. "Fine by me. What I'd really like to ask you both about is the missing family." When they both had blank expressions on their faces, I added, "There was a family with a five-year-old child that presumably disappeared from the hotel."

"Missing family?" the sheriff asked.

"Lois never told me anything about it," Bertha Anne said. "She's friends with my mother, and believe me, she usually spills her guts. Was this very recent?"

"I'm not sure exactly when, but yes. Seems like nobody is really concerned about the family. They might have been searching for Leister's gold."

GHOSTLY HIJINKS

The sheriff frowned now. "Oh, I see. That's not good at all. Word has it that whoever searches for that gold is never heard from again."

"That seems to be the recurring theme."

"I'm sorry, but I can't help you with that one. My mother never even mentioned that."

"And you never saw a family that would fit that description?"

"Nope. We don't get too many families with children in the saloon, but if it's Leister's gold that they're after, God help them. Not anyone I've ever heard of has come back alive from such a search."

That certainly wasn't what I wanted to hear. I had hoped to get some kind of clue, something that might help me find the family. "Does anyone have a clue where the gold might be located?"

"If we did, we'd have gone after it ourselves," the sheriff said.

We enjoyed the rest of our coffee in silence and it was obvious that finding the family might just be more difficult than I'd expected.

Chapter Eight

Eleanor and I finally made it back to the hotel since we weren't able to come up with any clues at the saloon and I was too tired to go anywhere else. Andrew and Mr. Wilson were still in the saloon of the hotel, but they left the card table with little prompting from us. We entered the dining room. Boy, was I starving since Eleanor and I hadn't had any lunch. As it was, I was wired after drinking the coffee.

Once we had placed our order, we sat in virtual silence since none of the men were speaking. I finally said, "Don't everyone speak at once."

"Sorry, Agnes. Mr. Wilson lost a good sum of money, but with my help he won it all back."

"Th-They're a bunch of no good cheaters," Mr. Wilson said.

"It might be part of a reenactment," I said. "In the Tumbleweed Saloon today, Eleanor and I saw a card game go to the birds and wound up with fists flying until the sheriff showed up."

"That sounds like fun. I wish I had gone with you instead of hanging out with Wilson all day."

"Y-You weren't saying that when you were flirting with that saloon girl, Patty," Mr. Wilson said with a wink.

I felt the anger go straight to my face as my cheeks burned. "Is that right, now?"

Andrew squeezed my hand and I laughed it off. "I better keep an eye on you, Andrew."

"Not to worry. I truly only have eyes for you. So, what were you girls up to today?"

"Oh, nothing much. We learned about the history of the hotel from the owner, Francine. Remember, the one I told you I'd dreamed about?" When his brow arched, I added, "The reenactment we saw today involved a sheriff that I also dreamed about. It seems like my dream is feeling more real all the time, except for seeing that little girl, Rebecca, in Room 109."

"Perhaps I was in too much of a rush to not believe you about the family. Patty told me all about the family and how they really were cash-strapped. I'm betting that they're destitute enough to go search for Leister's gold even."

"Did Patty mention where the gold might be located?"

"Nope. You get any information about it at the saloon?"

I shook my head. "I'm beginning to wonder if I'll ever get a break, or if finding this family might be as elusive as the gold."

Andrew squeezed my hand again. "I don't like to hear you talk like that, Agnes. Besides, since when do you listen to me or anyone else when you're on the trail of a mystery? This one is just a little more difficult, but I have faith that you'll be able to figure it out."

I sighed. "Thanks, Andrew. I really needed to hear that. Did you know that the owner, Francine, never even reported the family missing to the sheriff?"

"Really? That seems strange. Did they run out on the bill?"

"Yes, and I just feel that the sheriff should have been involved in some way."

"Did you speak to the sheriff yet?"

"Not yet. Francine assured us that she'd report their disappearance to the sheriff and I wanted to give her the opportunity to do so. I hardly want anyone to think that I'm a know it all."

"Which you totally are," Andrew said with a snicker.

I would have said more, but our dinner came. Grilled lamb, peas and baked potatoes were served, and although it wasn't what I'd call a gourmet meal, it certainly was tasty, and more tender than any meat I'd ever eaten. We had white wine with dinner and I welcomed the fruity taste since the caffeine from earlier had me too cranked up.

When we finally made it upstairs, I saw the yellow police tape over the door of Room 109, but I hardly gave it another thought. I didn't react when I saw Caroline talking with the ghostly shape of a man. I simply figured she was talking with Niles, the ghost she had told me about.

My head hit the pillow and I all but ignored the footsteps over my head, knowing that it was only Crazy Mary. Once I began to put a name to these spirits and learned more about them, the less scary they seemed, and that was my last thought as I fell into an exhausted sleep.

When I woke up, I had a crick in my neck. Massaging it out wasn't an option, and just my luck, no Andrew in sight. I gathered my bath supplies and made my way for the shared bathroom, but just as I was about to knock on the door, I heard hushed voices. "Hurry up, Mr. Wilson. I don't have all day now," Eleanor said, impatiently.

"It's not my fault. It's been a long time since I've done this," Wilson complained.

Grunts and groans ensued now. "It's not gonna fit," Wilson next said.

"Well, it did the last time."

Andrew came up behind me and whispered in my ear, "What's happening?"

"It's Mr. Wilson and Eleanor. I think they're getting freaky."

"Would you quit fumbling and just do it already," Eleanor snapped.

"I won't if you want to act like that." The door began to open and he said, "Do it yourself, then."

My eyes widened, as did Andrews. Our eyes locked on Mr. Wilson, who had his robe wrapped closely around his narrow frame. "Don't just stand there, help out Eleanor. I tried, but she wouldn't let me and now she's in a fix for sure."

"What?"

"Get your mind out of the gutter, old girl. Her zipper, Eleanor needs help with her zipper," he said as he trounced away and Andrew followed him, his laughter echoing up the hallway.

When I walked into the bathroom, Eleanor was indeed in an awful fix. She was bent over at the waist. Her arms were halfway in the sleeves of her sweater, one shoulder raised in a dangerous position, her other arm stuck backward, obviously stuck in the fabric.

"Oh, my. I'm afraid I don't know quite what to do."

"That's not what I want to hear. Help me out of this sweater. I feel faint."

I moved into action, trying to lift the sweater off one arm, until Eleanor winced. "Oh, bother. I should fetch a pair of scissors," I suggested. "Otherwise, you might just be stuck in there until dinnertime."

"No way. This is cashmere."

"Since when do you wear cashmere, or any sweater in this heat?"

"Because I wanted to, is all. Can't a girl look nice for her man?"

"Sure she can, but what size is this sweater?"

"It's a size twelve."

I tried not to laugh. "I thought you wore a size sixteen?"

"Oh, please get me out of this sweater. I don't care anymore. Run and get the scissors then."

"Are you sure you'll be okay?" I asked on my way to the door.

"Please hurry," was her response.

I hustled out the door and headed into the elevator since I didn't have any scissors in my suitcase. There was no way I'd be allowed to carry something like that on the airplane, so I'd left them at home.

Once I was on the first floor, I ran to the front counter. "Could I borrow a pair of scissors?" I asked Lois.

She looked at me in my pink ruffled bathrobe and asked, "Whatever for, and why are you wearing your bathrobe down here? We run a respectable hotel here, you know."

"Eleanor was trying to put on her sweater and it was the wrong size. So, she's stuck in it. If I don't cut her out of her sweater, and soon, she might just fall out on the floor. That won't look too good for the Goldberg, now will it?" I held out my hand until a pair of scissors appeared on my palm.

"Fine, but you bring them right back, you hear?"

I raced back to the elevator, ignoring a group of women who were just coming out of it, and also the gasps of indignation that I totally ignored as I went into the elevator and pushed the number three button.

Within minutes, I headed back into the bathroom, but instead of Eleanor still trapped in her clothing, she was putting her makeup on at the mirror.

"Eleanor? What happened? I-I th—"

"Well, I was stuck pretty good, but someone helped me out."

"Who?" I asked, searching the small bathroom.

"I'm really not sure, but he was a tall one. With a few cuts with his knife, I was free."

"Him ... knife? What on earth, Eleanor?"

"I'm not sure, but like I said, by the time I turned to see who it was, he was long gone—and the room was so cold."

"Weren't you scared when someone wielding a knife cut you out of your sweater?"

Poised to apply her red lipstick, she replied, "Actually, I was really hurting at the time so I just didn't care."

"You didn't get nicked, did you?"

"I don't think so." Eleanor lifted her bathrobe so that I could take a look underneath and her skin didn't have a mark on it, except for the plentiful moles she already had.

I let the fabric go and said, "That's so odd, and I'm just a little concerned. I mean, for all you know, a man came in here to hurt you, or a malevolent spirit."

"I'm not sure, but all I know is that I'm now free of that sweater. It's over there in the trash can if you want to take a look-see."

I pulled the remnants of her sweater out of the trash and examined the rips in the fabric that were long and jagged, with exposed threads. "You don't think The Cutter came in here, do you?"

"The Cutter?" Eleanor eased herself onto the closed toilet seat. "Th-That's not possible. I mean, he chased us out of the library just yesterday. Didn't you say that he always stays in the library?"

"I thought so, but if it's not The Cutter, then who else could it be?"

"Beats me, Agnes, but why not ask Caroline? Maybe she'll know."

Eleanor disappeared out the door and I took a bath, more nervous than ever. If The Cutter was just here once, what would be stopping him from coming back? I certainly didn't want a Psycho-type scene reenactment. Then I figured I was taking a bath, not a shower, so considered myself safe from that type of scenario.

How does one conjure a spirit? I thought, thinking of Caroline as I paced my room. Andrew wasn't here now and it would be the perfect time to talk to her, but I was at a loss as to how to proceed. I guess I should ask Caroline how it all works. It would be helpful if I could just utter a simple phrase and she magically showed up, but I guess things just don't work like that. I then decided to say out loud, "Caroline, where are you?"

GHOSTLY HIJINKS

Laughter began behind me and I whirled—there Caroline was lying down on the bed with her hands interlaced behind her neck.

"How long have you been there?"

"A few minutes. Ever since you started thinking about how to find me."

"I didn't think that exactly, but I'm happy that you're here now." I sank into a chair. "Something happened earlier and I just don't know what to make of it." I then told Caroline about what happened in the bathroom with Eleanor and how someone or something cut her out of the sweater she was trapped in.

"So, you never saw anyone come out of the bathroom when you went back there with the scissors?"

"No, and Eleanor said it was quite cold after her sweater was finally removed. Is it possible a ghost did the deed—helped Eleanor, I mean?"

Caroline sat up. "I'm not sure, but I suppose I could ask around. You said she was cut out of the sweater with a knife?"

"Yes, and my first thought was that it might be the—"

"Shhhh, don't say *his* name or *he* might show up."

I sighed. "I was under the impression that *he* stayed in the library."

"Just because that's where he's been, doesn't mean that's where he'll stay. Spirits aren't rooted to a particular spot, you know."

"You were once rooted back in East Tawas. You told me you were stuck to hang out on US 23 after you were ran down, remember? Until you decided to attach yourself to me."

"Hey, I never actually decided that. It's just what happened. I still haven't figured out how this dead thing works."

"Me, either, when it comes to you. So all I have to do is to think about you for you to appear?"

"Pretty much, unless something scary happens. Then I'm outta there like yesterday's news."

I frowned. "That's another thing. If you want to be part of the partnership, you can't be doing that. Eleanor and I might really need you and what good would it be if you won't stick around to help us out?"

"You're both pretty resourceful. Besides, I don't want to come between you and Eleanor."

"You won't. No offense, but Eleanor and I are thicker than molasses. There's just no way you'd ever be able to do that."

There was a knock at the door. Caroline flew into the dresser, and it took a few minutes before she was able to disappear completely. I had to chuckle a little at that and answered the door, but there was only a box sitting there on the floor. I picked it up and wondered if I should open it or not until Caroline appeared next to me. "I don't think this looks too dangerous," Caroline said. "Open it."

I shuffled inside. "You open it."

"Fine, then." She reached through the box and came back with a cowboy boot as the box popped open. "Like I said, harmless unless you want to use this boot for walking all over someone," she winked.

I waltzed over to the bed, feeling a bit foolish now. I pulled out western apparel in the form of a fringed vest and matching skirt that, along with the cowboy boots, would look very western indeed. I found an envelope and opened it, scanning the card that was inside with only the words, "Compliments of Francine Pullman."

Caroline read the card and said, "How neighborly of her."

"Indeed. I had the impression that I'd rubbed her the wrong way yesterday."

"If you did, she's over it."

Not wanting to offend Francine if I saw her today, I donned the clothing, which fit quite well. "What do you think?" I asked Caroline as I struck a pose.

Caroline clapped her hands. "Love it. I can't wait to see what your friends think of it."

GHOSTLY HIJINKS

"I hope you stay invisible to them while you do that. Andrew didn't take well to seeing the spirit in the library yesterday."

"I see. So he put a real scare into him, did he?"

"Sure did, but a spirit brandishing a knife is a pretty scary sight. He even slashed at Andrew."

"Oh, I see. I'm sure not looking forward meeting him."

I smiled at Caroline as we parted ways at the elevator, hoping that she'd actually meet Douglas and not leave me all alone with the angry spirit.

Chapter Nine

When I entered the dining room, I treaded lightly in my brand new cowgirl attire and I had to admit, I loved the feeling of the apparel. Luckily, I had a button-up white shirt to wear underneath the vest. I couldn't wait to see what Andrew thought about my new ensemble. Too bad Andrew didn't have any western apparel, too. I imagined that he'd look like quite fetching wearing black with a gun belt around his narrow waist.

After a few minutes of looking, I couldn't see Andrew at our regular table, but instead, there was a much larger table in its place.

Halfway there, I even spotted three older women that I didn't recognize until I stood at the table. The one in the middle smiled and said, "Well, Agnes, it sure looks like you fit in here with that western apparel."

I squinted. "Mrs. Barry, is that you?"

"Of course, and you remember Mrs. Peacock and Mrs. Canary, right?"

I nodded at the ladies. "Oh, but of course. Fancy meeting you ladies so far from Redwater, Michigan." Redwater is a small town in Michigan's thumb area that Eleanor and I had vacationed at before. "Is Birdy here, too?" I asked, indicating Mrs. Peacock's foul-mouthed Macaw bird.

"Oh, no. One of my neighbors is looking after Birdy. He'd never last through an airplane ride here," Mrs. Peacock said.

I smiled at Eleanor, who sauntered to the table. "I have western apparel, too," she said, showing off her denim skirt and matching shirt, lifting it just enough so I could see her cowboy boots.

"Well, obviously we must have made an impression on Francine yesterday when we met her. I'm so shocked she sent us some real authentic western apparel," I went on to say.

"I know, right? Where's Andrew and Mr. Wilson?" Eleanor asked the group of women.

"They haven't shown up yet, but I hope they are wearing western apparel, too. You'll look like perfectly matched couples then," Mrs. Barry said.

Since we didn't see the men coming, we took a seat just as the server brought over the coffee, winking at me. "I have a special coffee just for you, Agnes, compliments from the Tumbleweed Saloon. Bertha Anne brought it special just for you."

I had to still my racing pulse and wanted to do a happy dance. "Oh, and what did she bring Redd?"

"Hopefully not an STD. That woman has been chasing Redd for quite a time, but I have the sneaking suspicion that he's just not all that interested in her."

Just then, I caught sight of Redd sneaking out of the kitchen, a finger pressed against his lips in a shushing motion. The door whipped open and Bertha Anne asked, "Where are you going in such a hurry?"

"I-I'm late for a meeting," he said as he raced across the dining room and flew through the door leading to the back of the hotel.

Bertha Anne threw up her hands. "I just don't know what I'm doing wrong," she muttered as she walked by.

"You could act a little less eager," Mrs. Barry said. "Some men just don't like an aggressive gal."

"No? Well, I guess I could try that, but I swear that man is playing too hard to get. Do you know he's never even been married before?"

"Perhaps he's not intending to ever be, married I mean, if that's your plan," I said. "I just don't take Redd for a marrying man."

GHOSTLY HIJINKS

"That's such a disappointment. This town just doesn't have enough eligible bachelors."

"I can't imagine so. Why did you move here, then?"

"Oh, I don't know. I suspect Leister's gold, but the people around here won't even talk about it all that much. How am I ever going to figure out where it is if folks won't even talk about it?"

"Perhaps because they don't know."

"I guess, but at least more men will come to town with the Gold Rush Festival coming tomorrow," Bertha Anne said as she walked away.

"That's why we're here," Mrs. Barry said. "Best ribs in Nevada, they say."

"Oh, have you been here before, then?"

"Certainly have. Why else would we be here? Never heard about Leister's gold though. That's worth checking into."

"I wouldn't recommend doing that. There's a missing family in search of it, and Eleanor and I are doing our best to find them before they perish."

"Missing, you say. Are you two here on a case?" Mrs. Peacock asked.

"We didn't come here to investigate one, but it kinda fell in our laps."

"Sounds like business as usual," Mrs. Canary added.

We had our breakfast with the normal small talk about Mrs. Peacock's Macaw, Birdie, almost being taken by animal control after it escaped from its perch and nested in a tree near a playground, foul mouth and all.

I just about jumped straight out of my skin when Caroline snickered in my ear. "Meet me by the library door." And here I thought I'd like it better if she were invisible. Not so much.

"Hurry up, Eleanor. We should … er … look for our menfolk."

We said our goodbyes, promising to catch up with Mrs. Barry

and the bird sisters at another time, preferably before Mrs. Barry had slammed back too many beers as she had a wont to do.

Caroline was standing by the library, now in visible mode to us, as Eleanor and I joined her. "What's up?" I asked Caroline. "Did you ask the spirits if they were the ones who helped Eleanor earlier?"

"What?" Eleanor asked with whitened face. "So you think it really was a ghost that cut off my sweater for real?"

"Well, of course. Who else, since we're the only ones staying on the third floor?"

"Not for long," Caroline said. "Niles said that the hotel gets pretty booked up during the Gold Rush Festival."

I'm not sure I like the sound of that. It was hard enough to share the bathroom with four people as it was. "I see. So did you find out anything or not?"

"Actually, yes and no. I asked Niles, who vehemently denied it. He told me he tries his best to not interact with *live ones*, as he calls the living."

"How about Crazy Mary?"

"She denied it, too. Right before she threw me out of the attic and told me to never come back. I think she thinks Niles and I are an item."

"Oh, what makes you think that?"

"She told me is how. I tried to explain to her how she has it all wrong, but she's not the listening type. Niles told me that sums up Crazy Mary in a nutshell."

"Is it true that she murdered Niles and then took her own life here at the hotel?"

"Oh, I'm not sure. Niles never told me that, but I suppose it sounds about right. My own life was ended not too differently when my fiancé was upset that I was leaving him."

"Don't blame yourself. Nobody has the right to end anyone's life, no matter what they do."

GHOSTLY HIJINKS

"Niles assured me that he never betrayed Crazy Mary."

"And yet, he hasn't told you the whole truth as of yet. Be careful, Caroline."

"I plan to be, but I'm already a ghost. There's not much else Crazy Mary can do to me."

"This is nice and all, but why are we here now, Caroline?" Eleanor asked.

"We're going to ask Douglas if he was the one who helped you out earlier, Eleanor. He's the only spirit in the Goldberg Hotel that is known to wield a knife."

"I don't much care," Eleanor admitted. "And I sure as heck am not going back in that library. We barely escaped with our lives the last time."

"I assure you that won't happen this time. I won't allow Douglas to hurt either of you," Caroline said. "Please, Eleanor, come inside with me. We'll go in together as a brave front."

"I just don't see why?"

"Come on, Eleanor. I really need to know."

"Why?"

"Because if The C— I mean Douglas, has come upstairs once, I would like to know if he plans to do it again, is all."

"It will be okay, I promise I'll stick with you girls this time," Caroline said as the library door creaked open. She floated into the room with us following her.

"I don't think he's in here now," I said.

"Maybe we should come at another time," Eleanor said, as she made a mad dash to the door, but before she made it there, a black mist surrounded her and she screamed at the top of her lungs, with her palms out as if trying to push it away.

The mist backed off a few feet, and Douglas's ghostly formed appeared from it. "Please, stop screaming. It really grates on my nerves."

Eleanor clamped her mouth shut. "Oh, I-I'm sorry, but you scared me."

"Didn't mean to, dear lady. I'd hate to scare you away." He smiled, a jagged knife in his right hand.

"What if you put the knife down, then? You'd look a whole lot less scary that way," Eleanor suggested.

Douglas waltzed to the far side of the room. "I just can't. Believe me, I have tried, but it's all for naught."

"I see. Well, you poor dear. Were you the one who helped me out earlier upstairs?"

"Yes," he said, bashfully now. "I-I heard quite a commotion and your cries for help and I had to take a peek."

"A peek?" Eleanor exclaimed.

"I-I didn't mean it the way it sounds. I'm certainly not a pervert, you know."

Eleanor laughed nervously. "That certainly doesn't make me feel any better, but thanks for helping me out. You never even nicked me with that knife of yours."

"I've never tried to actually harm anyone I've slashed at before, but today I knew I had to help you out. Your cries for help were pitiful."

Eleanor's hands went to her hips. "Why do you do that anyway? Scaring folks like that just isn't right."

"I know. It's just that I just started a really good book and hate to be disturbed."

"Oh, what are you reading?" Eleanor asked, interested.

"*Moby Dick*. It's a great book with so much action and adventure, don't you think?"

"I've never read that book, but how about *The Adventures of Tom Sawyer*?"

"That's okay, but not as quite riveting as *Moby Dick*."

"What else do you have in this library to read?"

"Nothing current, unfortunately. There's not been a new book brought in here since the renovation, and most of the books that were already here had been here since before the fire that didn't enter the library."

"Perhaps if you hadn't scared folks away, they would have added to the library," I suggested with a curt nod.

"Nobody comes to Silver to read books. They're more concerned with touring the town and mine shafts."

"I suppose, but perhaps we should speak to Lois about bringing in new books. I'm sure you'd enjoy the new books they have these days."

"Or proper ligature, like Jack London. You'd love *Call of the Wild*," Eleanor said. "Have you ever read a western?"

"Yes, dear lady. Someone left a Louis L'Amour book in the dining room once."

"He's one of the best western writers if you like cowboy and Indian books," Eleanor said. "How about if you quit scaring folks out of here and we find you more currant books to read?"

"Only if you promise to come back, dear. It's been an eternity since I've had any real female companionship."

Eleanor blushed. "I'd love to, but I must be honest and tell you that I'm already taken. Engaged even," she showed Douglas her engagement ring.

"I see. Well, if you can tear yourself away from your man, I'd love the company sometime. Please," Douglas pleaded with her.

"Oh, I suppose, but right now we're trying to solve a mystery."

"Anytime, dear lady. As you know, I'm not going anywhere," Douglas said as he faded away.

Eleanor threw her shoulders back and strode out into the hallway. When the door opened, Lois hit the floor as she obviously had her ear pressed to the door in an effort to eavesdrop.

"Lois," I said. "What on earth are you doing on the floor?" I asked with a smile.

She clamored to her feet and adjusted her clothing. "You girls need to be more careful. You're gonna kill someone coming out of a door like that."

"I don't expect that will happen since most folks don't eavesdrop."

"Yes," Eleanor said. "Did you have a glass pressed to the door or what?"

"Of course not! I just heard someone scream and came to check out where it was coming from."

"That was me," Eleanor volunteered. "I think I saw a mouse in the library."

"If you stay too long in there, you'll find more than just a mouse. Haven't you heard the library is haunted by a madman?"

"What on earth?" I asked with a hand pressed against my bosom. "That's quite some accusation. Madman, indeed."

"No, really, it's true. Douglas Renny was a legendary gunslinger who murdered ten people in Virginia City alone. The U.S. Marshal finally hunted him down right here in the library, gunned him down, and ever since, his ghost lurks in the library. He carries a knife, you know."

"A knife? What kind of gunslinger carries a knife and not a gun belt?" I asked.

"How do you know what he wears and doesn't?" Lois asked. "Have you seen his ghost firsthand?"

I shook my head. "No, I just know a gunslinger wouldn't carry a knife if he was that much of a killer. Are you sure you even heard that story right?"

"I've lived in Silver for twenty years now, and you're the only person that has dared question me. Who were you girls talking to in the library?" she pressed.

"Nobody," we chimed. "Except for each other," I added.

"There's no need to lie now. I heard at least two other voices."

"I don't think so, but if you're concerned, perhaps you should go into the library to check it out for yourself," I said, knowing full well that she'd never go in there.

"Are you plain loco? I'm not going in there. Didn't you hear me? The library is haunted."

"It is, now?" Francine came waltzing up with Redd, who looked like he'd rather be elsewhere since he wouldn't make eye contact with us.

"There weren't any ghosts when we were in there," I said. "And Lois accused us of lying."

"Lois, is this true?" Francine said with a disapproving look on her face. "How many times have I told you to not anger the guests?"

"Fine, but if nobody but those two were in there, how come I heard other voices?"

"Perhaps because we were reading one of William Shakespeare's plays."

"Sure were," Eleanor added. "I was Juliet and Agnes was Romeo," she snickered.

I cocked a brow at that, but continued to play along. "She always makes me be the man. It's tiring, really," I said with a wink.

"I don't care about any of this, really," Francine said. "Lois, get back to work. You've kept guests waiting at the desk."

Lois shot us an angry look, but we never let on that there was a bit of truth in what she had said. "Thanks for the western apparel, Francine. It was very kind of you."

"You're quite welcome, and I wanted to make up for how I treated you at my house yesterday. You were right about the missing family. I really should have reported it to the sheriff straight off. I guess I just didn't want word to get around that the Goldberg had another family disappear in the middle of the night. The last ones, the Thompsons from what I can recall, disappeared under the exact same circumstances. Unfortunately, that family was found dead in a canyon nearby with mining equipment. I really wish folks would not come to Silver thinking that Leister's gold is real. There's simply no proof that it is. It's a legend that has been told to tourists as a form of entertainment. I don't even know if there ever was a Peyton Leister ever living in Silver during the gold rush days."

"That's sure a bold statement. There must be some truth to it, or why would folks still come to Silver looking for gold?"

"For the Gold Rush Festival, of course. It's a big draw, but once most of them realize just how rough the terrain is around here, they give up on that notion. Anyway, that's not what I came here for. I wanted to tell you that I told the sheriff what I knew about the missing family. Thanks for allowing me to do that before you jumped into anything prematurely."

I wanted to say so many things, like it just might be too late for that family now, or how bad it made her look for not reporting it sooner, and only after I started asking questions about them.

"What's the family's name again?" I asked.

"I don't think it's a good idea to tell you. The sheriff wouldn't like me to tell anyone since he's now actively investigating."

"That's fine, then. I'll ask him myself," I said as I turned to leave in search of the men.

"I assure you, there's really no need for that."

I whirled and said, "And I assure you that I'll do everything in my power to bring that family safely home, and nothing you can say will stop Eleanor and me."

"What qualifies you to poke around?"

"Eleanor and I have investigated many crimes back home, with success, I might add. Unless you have a reason to try and stop us, we'll be on our way now to find our menfolk so we can enjoy our last day before the Gold Rush Festival begins."

Francine's mouth gaped open, but she clamped it shut and I was internally grateful, since I didn't want to outright accuse her of wrongdoing right now—not until I had solid evidence that would point to her, that is.

Ghostly Hijinks

Chapter Ten

Eleanor and I searched upstairs for Andrew and Mr. Wilson, but when they weren't up there, we proceeded back down in the elevator, ran back to the dining room, and then checked the saloon until the saloon girl, Patty, told us they were outside waiting for the parade to start.

Eleanor and I hustled outside beneath the overhang, finally spotting Andrew and Mr. Wilson. Andrew about knocked me out with his white western shirt and matching pants with metal rivets that were fastened to his shirt pocket and all along the sides of the legs of his trousers. He also had a gun belt around his waist with a pistol. "Let me guess. You must be the good guy," I said as I walked up.

"He sure is, and I'm the bad guy," Mr. Wilson said with a cracking voice. He wore all black with a long-sleeved shirt and pants, and as he walked toward us, spurs struck the clapboard porch with a jangle of metal. He also had a gun belt around his waist with a pearl-handled revolver. I sure bought into the idea that both of them were every inch western men.

Mr. Wilson let out a whistle, or his version of one with way too much wind and not enough whistle, but I got the idea.

I fanned my face in feigned embarrassment. "Was that for little ole us?" I asked.

Eleanor played along and took ahold of my arm. "Agnes, don't talk to the likes of him. He's an outlaw."

"Yes, but he's sort of cute, don't you think," I said, nudging Eleanor in the ribs. She then burst into laughter.

"I can't believe it, Mr. Wilson. You look like a real outlaw from one of those Old Western movies," Eleanor gushed.

"He'd better tow the line with you ladies, or I'll put this six shooter to good use," Andrew said as he tapped the silver sheriff's badge he wore. "You sure look quite fetching today, Agnes. I don't think I've ever seen you in a skirt before—either of you, actually."

"Thanks. I think. So what's going on out here?"

"There's supposed to be a parade," Mrs. Barry said as she held her beer glass tightly in her right hand.

"We just love the Gold Rush Festival," Mrs. Peacock said, fluttering her eyelashes at Mr. Wilson who sidled up next to Eleanor when her eyes narrowed slightly.

"I thought that didn't start until tomorrow," I said.

"The parade is always the day before," Mrs. Peacock said.

I heard what sounded like a gun going off as two men raced their horses up the street, scarves tied around their faces, concealing their identities from everyone. One man was holding a woman who had been thrown over one of their horses. I bit a fist even though I figured it was just part of the show, but the woman kicked and screamed so much that it seemed very real. Sheriff Wilford appeared in the middle of the street, pointing his rifle at the outlaws, who shouted, "Move out of the way, Sheriff, or this gal's life won't be worth a plug nickel."

"You let Miss Bertha Anne go, or else."

"Ain't gonna do that. We're ransoming her to her father. Peyton will be forced to show us where he hid the gold bars for sure then."

Peyton? As in Peyton Leister? This didn't sound much like a legend if they're using it as part of their reenactment.

"Please, take her out of town and never bring her back," Redd whispered to me with a chuckle. "That way I'll have some peace from her advances."

I pursed my lips. What a stubborn man this Redd was. "I don't think you mean that. She seems like a real nice lady."

"If she were a lady, I might give her half a chance, but ladies don't chase after men."

"Perhaps not in your generation they didn't, but times they have changed and Berta Anne has no other prospects."

Redd's brow furrowed, and instead of sticking around, he went back inside.

"What's his deal?" Eleanor asked. "Most men would be happy to have a lovely lady like that pursuing him."

"Not when it develops into stalking," Andrew said. "Word is that she calls Redd like twenty times a day."

That certainly wasn't good. "Perhaps I should have a chat with the girl."

Two more horses came up in full steam with men in white, surrounding the bad guys, who let Bertha Anne go. She ran into the sheriff's arms as the men were apprehended and taken into the jailhouse across the street. Applause were heard at the reenactment and it took a few minutes for the sheriff to pry Bertha Anne's fingers from his shirt.

"Yup, she's definitely a stalker," Eleanor said.

A band played a lively tune and passed us by, fully intent on playing their music while we all tapped our feet in time. Next was a wagon with clowns on it, tossing candy to children who lined the other side of the street.

Many more wagons passed by, some of which had gold rush era looking men who hooted and hollered that they just found the mother lode, holding huge rocks in their hands that were painted gold. Other wagons represented the many businesses in Silver, from the Tumbleweed Saloon that had a wooden keg of beer on their wagon, to one with provisions that a prospector might need from the Willington General Store, with Glenda O'Shay sitting on it. Next was the wagon carrying a banker counting money and weighing gold nuggets on a scale with magnifying glasses on his face.

All in all, it gave us a representation of what Silver might have been like back in the gold rush days. When the small parade was over, we all packed into the saloon of the hotel. In attendance was Badass Bart, who was telling everyone about how the merchants made more money than the prospectors did by overpricing their wares since most came to town with only the clothes on their backs.

"That's just awful. No wonder the Willington General Store is still in business," I said. "Can't blame them, I suppose, since there wasn't anyone stopping them. Folks have a right to make a living."

"True, but not on the backs of prospectors or miners," Eleanor said.

Bart massaged his beard. "Not to worry, dear lady. This was only a glimpse into Silver's past. I sure wish the gold hadn't run dry. Silver was such a booming town at one time."

"Really?" I asked. "Like, how many people actually lived here?"

"About twenty thousand. You outta take a look at the cemetery on the other side of town and check it out. I think you might be surprised."

I nodded, inhaling the scent of the beer that was handed to me. "Oh, Andrew. You should know that I can't stand this stuff."

"More for me," Mrs. Barry said. "Be a dear and slide your glass this away."

I smiled, doing as she asked. When I straightened my back, I caught sight of Sheriff Bradley over at the jailhouse and I nudged Eleanor. "Let's head on over to the jailhouse. We have some investigating to do."

We strolled across the street, sidestepping the horse poop that a man with a broom and trashcan was trying to clean up.

I stared up at the "Jail" sign and led the way into the jailhouse. I froze in my tracks at the group of men doing shots, and Eleanor plowed into me. "Really, Agnes?"

GHOSTLY HIJINKS

Sheriff Bradley wasn't even here. Had he slipped out the back? "Sorry to disturb you fellas, but I was hoping to speak with the sheriff." Sheriff Wilford stepped forward. "Oh, not you. I meant the real sheriff," I said.

Wilford grabbed the phone and made a call, and said, "Oh, Cliff, there's someone to see you."

Heels scratched across the floor and a sigh was heard as a man's heavy feet caused the floor to creak, making way to greet us, but he wasn't the sheriff. This man needed a shave and burped—the smell of alcohol quite strong. Seemed to me that he should be in the jail cell, sleeping it off, not in what I suspected was the sheriff's office.

I stared at the men who were part of the reenactment and not a one of them were smiling, but the fake sheriff had a smirk on his face.

"Aren't you fellas supposed to be in jail for kidnapping?" Eleanor asked with a snicker.

"It's darn uncomfortable in there. Would you like to see firsthand?" one of the men asked.

"Sure ain't," the drunk said, lowering himself into a chair. "When the sheriff isn't around these men let me stretch my legs."

"No need explaining yourself, Clarence. These ladies might just tell the sheriff," one of the men said.

"Oh, Wild Bill, I'm sure they won't do that. They look so nice, and the tall one reminds me of my mother."

I straightened my back at that insult. Why, Clarence looked nearly my age.

"Oh, did you like your mother?" I asked stalling for time.

His lips wrinkled up. "Not really. She's an evil bitch—pardon my French, ma'am."

I gulped, taken completely aback with the words that flew out of Eleanor's mouth as her eyes lit up. "Oh, can we really see the inside of the jail cell?"

115

"I-I don't think that's a good idea, Eleanor."

"Sure can," Wild Bill said. "If you don't mind the dust, that is." We were led into a jail cell, and stood there as the iron-barred door slid open. "Step inside, and I'll close the door so you can get a real feel for how it felt way back in the gold rush days."

Eleanor took ahold of my hand and yanked me inside. I practically had a heart attack when the door was indeed slammed shut behind us. I gripped the bars. "Okay, enough fun now, boys. Let us back out. I'm claustrophobic," I implored them.

Wild Bill glanced around the room. "Has anyone seen the key?"

"You know there's no key," Clarence said. "That's why the sheriff never closes the door."

The men laughed and I felt a wild panic start. "That's not funny, boys."

"Sure ain't," Clarence said.

The men moved to leave and I shouted, "Sheriff Wilford, you're not going to leave us, are you?"

"Sorry, I'm not a real sheriff, remember? Name's Jeff," he said as he left with the rest of the men who were each slapping each other on the backs.

Clarence had a long face when he stared at us. "Why on earth would you willingly walk in a cell like that fer?"

I stared over to Eleanor who I just wanted to give a kick, but neither of us were the age that we could handle something like that. I scanned the room, sizing up the small bunk and bucket in the corner. "What's that bucket for?" I asked Clarence.

"It's the bathroom."

I about hurled and moved to the bunk and sat down, jumping back up when something poked me where the sun don't shine. "What on earth is that bunk made of?"

"Straw, I think. I told you it wasn't comfortable in there."

I hustled to the bars when I saw a rodent scurry past. "This isn't funny now. Tell me there really is a key to this cell."

Clarence's hands moved in the air as he threw his hands up in the air. "Sure, there's a key. I was just kidding when I said there wasn't one. Sheriff Bradley has it with him at all times. You'll just have to wait until he comes back." He then got up and yawned. "I'll go back in the sheriff's office. It's much more comfortable in there."

When Clarence disappeared, I began to bang my head on the bars softly. "Some fix you got us into this time," I said to Eleanor. "Not one of your brainier moments."

"Sorry," Eleanor said. "Boy, this cell sure is small. Do you think Clarence was just kidding about what they use the bucket for? I mean, it seems pretty inhuman to have a prisoner use a bucket to do their business in."

"How about we don't talk about having to use the bathroom, because I hafta pee."

"Didn't you realize you had to go before we came over here? I swear, it seems like you would have gone back at the hotel."

I tried to get my mind off of my need to use the bathroom and quickly. "I didn't have to go, then. I think I have a nervous bladder. Let's talk about something else."

"What do you want to talk about, then?"

"Francine, for one," I began. "I can't help but wonder if she's hiding something. I also can't shake the feeling that she knows more about the missing family than she's letting on."

"True, and suddenly she comes up with the name of another missing family, the Thompsons. Do you think she's trying to make us think that the missing family is dead?"

"Seems that way, and she certainly doesn't want us talking to the sheriff, either."

"Of course, that Lois seems like she might be hiding something, too. She's certainly unfriendly."

"Well, being unfriendly hardly qualifies someone for guilt, but

I don't care all that much for how she's treated us. Ever since she found out we weren't married, it's been all downhill."

I checked the bars now, to see if any of them were loose at least, and when I found one that was, I worked it back and forth until it dropped to the door, clanging as it fell. I glanced around the small space of the room. There was a very worn desk with a matching chair that one would sit to watch over the jail cell. No computer in sight or anything modern, but there was a black, rotary-dial phone that Sheriff Jeff had used to call the real sheriff.

Out of boredom, I gazed at the walls. There were many holes with what looked like bullets lodged in the wood. I imagined a shootout occurring here as outlaws tried to free their gang. Just like what might occur in an old western movie.

Eleanor and I decided to rest on the bunk, being careful not to lean against the wall, and nodded off to sleep.

I woke with a start as the door slammed open and we heard a man's throat clear. "Agnes Barton, what on earth are you doing in there? I've been worried that the ground had sucked you two up," Andrew said with a frown. "It's almost dinnertime now."

The thought of food launched my stomach into growling. I nudged Eleanor awake. "Eleanor wanted to see the inside of the jail cell, and those men who were doing the reenactments locked us in here, telling us there wasn't a key. That phony Sheriff Wilford—he's an actor, you know. Anyway, he supposedly called the real sheriff to tell him we were waiting for him here, but he never showed. I have my doubts that he called him at all."

"Perhaps I should go look for him myself."

"Oh, geez. I have to pee so bad and there's only a bucket in here to do that."

Andrew's nostrils flared at that. "We'll see about that." He spotted the bar that was on the floor. "How did that happen?"

"I managed to find a loose one and worked on it a bit, but neither Eleanor nor I can fit though a crack that size."

Andrew checked the bars and took ahold of one, turning it back and forth until it, too, fell to the floor with a crash. The door behind Andrew swung open and Sheriff Bradley bellowed, "What are you doing, man?"

"Trying to get my fiancée and her friend out of this cell. Those reenactment men locked them in here, and they've been trapped in there for a good part of the day. I have half a mind to sue," Andrew shouted at the sheriff.

"I had no idea."

"Sheriff Wilford didn't call and tell you that we came here to speak with you?"

"Call me how?"

"Well, that phone over there," Eleanor said. "We heard him make the call."

"For one, I haven't been anywhere near a phone, and for two, cell phones don't work in Silver because of the mountains in the area." He then pulled out his keys and opened the cell, sliding the door open, staring angrily at the fallen bars. "I'll speak with Jeff about keeping you locked up here. He knew full well where I was, but honestly, he usually doesn't do things like this, I assure you."

I danced from one leg to the other. "Do you happen to have a bathroom I could use? I've been holding it for hours now."

He opened his office door, and shook his head at Clarence leaning back in his chair, his feet on his desk, sporting holes in his socks, snoring away. He pointed out another door. "Right though there."

I raced to the bathroom and came back five minutes later, feeling so much better. "Why isn't there a toilet in the cell?"

"Because I let whoever I have locked up use my bathroom. As

you can see, some of them take unfair advantage." He yanked his chair back and Clarence threw out his arms to steady himself as the chair wobbled, nearly tossing him to the floor.

"What you doing that fer, Sheriff?"

"You know full well why. Your feet smell bad enough to kill a skunk, and you know that you're not supposed to leave the cell."

"I can't help it that I like your chair better than that sorry bunk in the cell."

"This ain't the Goldberg Hotel, you know."

"I-I know, but—"

"No buts about it. Go on home now, and I had better see you walk that way, too. And this time, stay away from the saloons."

Clarence pouted and made for the door, and from the sheriff's window, I could see him head toward the cemetery. "So I take it this is a weekly occurrence?"

The sheriff took out a can of air freshener and sprayed the office and chair, moving it aside and rolling out a leather one from a closet, easing himself into it. "That's better. I always change chairs because more times than not, Clarence winds up in my office when I'm not here."

"Is that normal? Seems like you wouldn't want anyone snooping in your office."

"Clarence doesn't do anything like that. When I pick him up, he barely can walk. I really wish he'd find a hobby or a woman, but I can't much see a woman putting up with his drinking."

"So he's not married, then?"

"He was once, but she left long ago. What can I help you ladies with? I suspect you had a good enough reason to stop by here, and I sure as heck know it didn't have anything to do with taking up time in the jail cell."

I took a seat near his desk and Eleanor took another. "Go along back to the hotel, Andrew," I said. "Eleanor and I have a few questions for the sheriff."

"We wouldn't want to bore you with unnecessary details," Eleanor added. "Just boring investigator questions."

"I think I'll stick around all the same."

"Go ahead if you want, but what of Mr. Wilson? What if he's in the saloon again playing cards? I'd hate to see him lose any more money," Eleanor said. "And I don't want Mrs. Barry or those strange bird sisters moving in on my man."

The sheriff cocked a brow. "Bird sisters? That's a new one."

"Yes, Mrs. Peacock and Mrs. Canary," I said. "They're also from Michigan."

"Oh, I thought you were trying to be funny."

I smiled, staring up at Andrew who finally threw up his arms and said, "Fine," then left without saying another word.

"Sorry," I said. "He's an attorney and doesn't much like Eleanor and me investigating crimes."

Sheriff Bradley smiled. "Oh, and what crime do you mean, exactly? Not a new one, I hope. Until you ladies showed up, I've never even handled a murder investigation."

"Murder?" I asked with widened eyes. "You mean the family that's missing?"

"No. I thought you were talking about the body you found in Room 109 of the Goldberg."

I leaned forward in my chair, the wheels of the chair creaking under my shift in weight. "How can you be so certain that's it's murder, Sheriff Bradley?"

"Call me Cliff," the sheriff said. "Since you've come to town, I've had to do some checking on you and found out you both are quite the investigators, but it seems that this body is quite old. The anthropologist hasn't sent me his report quite yet, but I strongly suspect that the remains have been there for over a hundred years. There is evidence that a rope was used to tie the woman down, so I do believe the woman was murdered."

"So was an autopsy done?"

"Yes. The pathologist came here yesterday, and the woman was also pregnant. The baby was petrified inside the remains, or part of it."

I took in a haggard breath. "Oh, how awful. So does the pathologist think the woman had miscarried and then died?"

"Hard to tell since the remains are quite old. If the woman was murdered, it's fair to say that whoever killed the woman is long gone now."

"You mean dead, don't you Cliff?" I asked.

"Yes, but I'd sure like to put a timeline together with the date of the remains when I find out for certain."

"I wonder if the woman is Elizabeth, the prostitute that Jessup Goldberg had supposedly locked away. We heard that she was pregnant."

"That's a legend, all right, but there's no proof there was ever an Elizabeth or that she ever stayed at the hotel in Jessup's lifetime."

"Then there's Wilfred Pullman, Francine's great-grandfather. She told us a story about how he told her father, Barry, to never go into Room 109."

Cliff rubbed the back of his neck. "What concerns me the most is that we might never learn the true identity of the woman, or who was really responsible for her death."

"What bothers me the most is that it might have been covered up all these years. I mean, why would Wilfred tell his family to never go into Room 109? Did Francine go into that room and know about the remains? And if she did, why would she keep it concealed all these years?"

"All good questions, but I suppose it would put a serious black mark on the Pullman family if Wilfred was indeed responsible for the woman's death."

"I can't imagine that should matter, but I guess I can see why

Francine might have an interest to conceal it. But first, we'd have to prove she did indeed conceal it."

The sheriff stood and made way for his coffee maker and made a pot, walking back to his chair, easing himself onto it. "Is that all you came here for, then?"

"No," I said, "but thanks for sharing that bit of information with us."

"I know you'd never let this rest otherwise, and I really don't feel like being bothered constantly."

"So Francine reported the family missing that disappeared from the Goldberg Hotel?"

"Yes, and I was really upset about it, too. They've been gone four days now and that's too much of a head start if they have gotten themselves lost."

"Could you give me the family's name? I'd like to find out more about them."

"You should know I'm not supposed to do that, Agnes"

"I know, but—"

"That's a long 'but' there."

"Listen, Sheriff, Agnes really has to know. She had this dream about this family and feels personally involved."

Cliff ran a hand through his hair. "I guess it doesn't matter all that much now. I'd sure like any help I can get. The last thing I want to happen is to have another family dead in the desert." My heart almost skipped a beat as the sheriff said, "Trisha and Aaron Jameson were a young couple with a vivacious daughter, Rebecca."

"Was she about five?" I asked.

"Sure was. I still can't believe they're missing, too. They were very down on their luck and I'm not sure where they heard about Leister's gold, but they did. Brought mining equipment with them, too. When the guide at the Lemon Pine Mine reported to me that they forced themselves past the allowed tour, I went out there and made them leave. Luckily, they hadn't gone far because that mine is mighty dangerous."

"I bet that sure made them mad."

"That is an understatement. They were very distraught over the whole deal. When I gazed into Trisha's eyes, I saw desperation mirrored in them. It really had quite an effect on me, but there just wasn't anything I could do for them. If I knew where that gold was, they'd be the ones I'd tell. Sometimes it's so easy to just shut off your emotions, but I just couldn't do it regarding them. It killed me to tell them that Leister's gold was only a legend, but I just didn't want to see their corpses in the desert getting picked over by vultures. I had to tell them the truth, no matter how much I knew it would hurt them."

My heart was about to break for sure now at the sheriff's genuine admittance. "I just don't understand. If Leister's gold is just a legend, then why are they using it in the Gold Rush Festival parade today?"

"That's Francine's doing. She thinks it's good for Silver to have a legend like that."

"So was there ever really a Peyton Leister?"

"According to his tombstone at the cemetery."

"Why does Francine have so much power in this town?"

"Because she has the most money in town, I suspect. Her family started the festival years ago and it's good for business. I just hope nobody gets a mind to take it upon themselves to look for the gold bars."

I stood and stretched. "Thanks, Sheriff. I so appreciate you sharing your information, and I promise that we'll keep what you told us to ourselves." I stared over to where Eleanor still sat. "Isn't that right, Eleanor?"

"Oh, yes. Whatever Agnes says goes for me." She grimaced for a moment and asked me, "Can you help me up, Agnes?"

I helped Eleanor up and we left. "I sure hope they have something left over for us to eat. It's past seven now," I said.

Chapter Eleven

When we strode into the dining room, it was completely empty. I waltzed up to Bonnie, who was clearing tables, and asked, "Did we miss dinner?"

"I was wondering where you girls were. Yes, the cooks left for the night." When we both sighed, she added, "I'll see what I can rustle up."

Eleanor and I watched as Bonnie disappeared into the back. "Somehow, I envision Bonnie coming back with a peanut butter and jelly sandwich," I said.

"At this point, I don't even care."

Bonnie carried a tray with two plates, setting them down. "Redd's going to be so mad when he finds out that I snatched his dinner out of the fridge."

"I don't want to take his dinner away from him," I said. "We can just have a peanut butter sandwich."

"Don't be silly, Agnes. You're a guest, and I won't see any guest going to bed hungry."

Eleanor and I dug into the prime rib and baked potatoes that we shared. I felt bad about Redd, but I was just so hungry and felt like my blood sugar had done a tailspin downward. It was so eerily quiet with just Eleanor and me in the dining room, and I shivered as I felt a chill, more so when I knew what that might just mean—that a ghost was nearby or already in the room with us.

"Caroline, is that you?" I whispered.

"Now you call her. Why didn't you try that when we were stuck in a jail cell?"

"Why didn't you?"

"Because she only answers to you, Agnes."

"I don't see her like that. She's a free spirit in more ways than one. I don't ever want to mistreat her, or take her for granted. She was kind enough to go into the library with us earlier."

"That's true and I didn't mean any disrespect. It's just that I wish she was around more when we really needed her, is all."

"Me, too, but I'm just not so sure how to get her to show up when I need her all of the time."

"Maybe you should ask her about that sometime."

"I already have, actually, and she told me to say her name or think about her, but so far that hasn't always worked out in my favor."

"You can't blame Caroline completely. Not unless you called her and she never came."

"True, and I never even thought about calling her when we were locked up. Sometimes I forget about this gift of mine, or wish that it would go away."

Eleanor took a drink of her wine that Bonnie had dropped off a few minutes ago. "I wouldn't go that far. When it comes to gifts, seeing ghosts isn't the worst one, like earlier today when we were actually able to have a civilized conversation with Douglas."

"Are you telling me that it didn't weird you out just a little bit that he cut you out of that sweater that you were stuck in?"

"A little, but I was just so happy to be free of it that it didn't matter all that much. What could he do to harm me, anyway?"

All I could think about was Douglas's jagged knife, but instead, I said, "I think Douglas likes you, Eleanor."

"What?" she blushed. "Naw, not a chance."

"He seemed quite intent to speak to you," I said. "But he's lonely,

I bet, and hasn't talked with a woman for possibly over a hundred years."

"True, and we should find a way to get him more books to read. If he's been dead since 1800-something, I bet he's already read every book in that small library, probably more than once," Eleanor said.

"We'll have to do that just as soon as we can," I said.

"Do what?" Andrew asked as he came up behind us.

"Stock the library with more current books."

Andrew's brow arched. "I don't know what for. There's a rather nasty ghost in there—one who carries a knife, don't forget."

"Oh, Douglas isn't all that bad, just a tad misunderstood," Eleanor said.

"And how would you know that?"

"Because Agnes and I chatted with Douglas earlier today. Agnes thinks he has a little crush on me," Eleanor gushed.

Andrew's eyes widened. "Is that right now? Well, I'd feel much better if the two of you stayed out of that library. It's not like you can trust a spirit." Andrew had a pained expression on his face. "I'm not exactly sure why I just said that, but it was way easier when I'd never seen a ghost."

"I know just what you mean, Andrew. That's why I told Caroline to never reveal herself to you."

Andrew eased himself into a chair. "So, what's this Caroline really like?"

"She's a real nice young lady. She died in the 1930s sometime. Her fiancé ran her over with his car when she left him."

"I meant what's she like as a person ... or ghost?"

"She's nice, like I said, but a little shy when something scary happens."

"That a shocker, but I can't say I blame her. I'd like to disappear when something dangerous happens, too." He laughed.

I forked in another morsel of my prime rib, my taste buds

humming a happy tune. Once I swallowed, I said, "I'm so bushed that I just know I'll sleep like the dead."

"Agnes Barton, don't you dare say something like that, and in a haunted hotel, no less," Eleanor said.

I jumped as I heard a loud boom nearby. "What on earth," I said.

"Relax. It's probably the fireworks that were set to go off at dusk."

"But it was only seven o'clock when we came back from the jailhouse."

"Are you sure your watch is right? Because it was around eight, then," Andrew said.

"Okay, fine. It can't even be dark outside yet."

"It gets darker here earlier than back home, Agnes."

Eleanor pushed herself away from the table, and stood. "I'm heading outside, then. I'd hate to miss the fireworks."

"Go on ahead. I'll be there just as soon as I finish my dinner."

"Suit yourself, Agnes," Eleanor said as she took Andrew's arm, leaving me to my thoughts.

Seriously, I really wished that I could just crawl upstairs without anyone noticing. I really was tired and I didn't know how long I'd be able to handle this heat.

After the last of my dinner was finished, I made way for the front door, but froze as I neared the front desk. Two men with guns and scarves covering their faces were threatening Lois. "Hand over the map, or else."

"I-I don't know what you're talking about. What map?"

A loud belch escaped my lips and I grimaced as one of the men now pointed his gun at me. "Hey, you. Get over here, real quiet-like."

I looked behind me, pointing at my chest. "Who … me?"

"Yes, you. Get moving before the fireworks are over. We don't want any more company, if you catch my drift."

I shuffled over there, wishing I had gone outside with Andrew and Eleanor. "Is this another reenactment?" I asked Lois, who vehemently shook her head.

"Hand over your purse, real quick-like."

"I don't have any money," I said, "This place took the last of it."

"Why do the old bags always cause us so much trouble?" one of the men asked, as he jerked the strap of my purse. I frowned when he had my bag in his hand and opened the zipper, taking out a handful of twenties. "I thought you didn't have any money?"

"Oh, well, I guess I just forgot is all. We old bags don't have the best of memories."

"Get behind the counter and help that woman look for the map."

I held my hands up as I dragged my feet all the way behind the counter, searching the shelves, but there was nothing more than receipts on them. "I don't see any map."

"Show her where the map is, or that old lady gets a slug in her noggin."

Lois grimaced. "I hardly know the woman, so why would I care if you popped her full of lead?"

I narrowed my eyes. "Perhaps because you'll have to clean up the blood."

"Good point, but I just don't know what map they're referring to."

A bag was tossed to me. "Empty the register and fill the bag. I'm getting mighty impatient."

"Why do I have to do it? I don't even work here, she does."

"Because she's gonna look for the map is why," one of the men whispered loudly.

"I already told you, I don't know what map you're talking about."

I eyed the brochures on a shelf behind Lois. "Oh, the map," I said, hitting my forehead with a palm. "It's right over there, remember, Lois?" I said with a wink that only she could see.

"Oh, yes. Don't just stand there. Give the men the map."

I hit the no sale button on the register. "I can't. I'm filling the bag, remember?" I kept hitting the button, but nothing happened. "I can't seem to open the register."

"That's because we're not allowed to do a no sale. You'll need a key to open the register."

"What are you waiting for? Open that damn register, already."

"Oh, I can't do that. Once the no sale key has been hit, the owner will have to come to open the register."

One of the gunmen, palm slapped his head. "And she's where, exactly?"

"Home, I suspect, but I'd be happy to tell her to come straight down here. I'll be sure to tell her you fellas are in a hurry."

I smiled. "Sounds like a plan."

One of the robbers glanced toward the front door and hissed, "Just give us the map already."

I waltzed over, took a brochure and with a sharpie quickly scrawled a map connecting the various businesses in town with a huge X on the cemetery out of the robber's line of sight. I then brought the map to the men who snatched it out of my hand and raced into the back.

"Good thinking, Agnes."

"I'm just glad they left—too bad it was with my purse, though. All of my identification was in there."

"Not to worry," Lois said as she picked up the phone and called the sheriff, but hung up without speaking. "He didn't answer."

"He's probably not in his office. He's most likely outside watching the fireworks. I'll go fetch him."

When I raced outside, fireworks lit up the night sky and Andrew grabbed ahold of my hand. "It's about time you got here. Isn't it beautiful?" he said.

I tugged my hand away, spotting Sheriff Bradley on the opposite side of the street. I raced across the street and whispered into the sheriff's ear, "I was just robbed inside the Goldberg Hotel."

GHOSTLY HIJINKS

He escorted me back to the hotel and made his way inside. Once we were inside, he asked, "Robbed, how?"

"When I was going outside for the fireworks, two gunmen were threatening Lois. They disappeared out back. Might even still be here for all I know."

The sheriff took one look at Lois' face and asked, "Are you okay, Lois?"

"Ruffled up a little, I suppose, but they took off with Agnes's purse."

"Did either of you see where they went?"

We shook our heads, and Andrew joined us and took me into his arms. "Oh, Agnes. I should never have left you in the dining room alone."

"The robbery didn't happen in the blasted dining room. It happened right here," Lois said with a curt nod.

"She's right. They were threatening Lois, demanding a map from her."

Sheriff Bradley had apparently sucked in a huge amount of air the way he pushed it out of his chest with a huge huff. "Map? That's the last thing I need to worry about, more treasure hunters."

"Perhaps you should gather a group of men to search the hotel for these men. They might still be here, man," Andrew said.

"They stole my purse," I said sadly. "It was just awful. They just jerked it right out of my hands."

The sheriff went back outside and came back with a group of ten men who disappeared in various directions, with Andrew now accompanying them. I felt a chill come over me and Caroline appeared and motioned me toward the library door. "Listen."

I pressed my ear to the door and heard high-pitched screams, stifling a laugh.

"What is it?" Lois asked, from behind me.

"I think the robbers are in the library with The Cutter."

"Oh, my," she said.

I opened the door and strode into the library, retrieving my purse that was lying on the floor, my money next to it. When I searched the library, Douglas, or The Cutter as he was known, had a knife pressed to the throat of one robber, with the other one on the floor under Douglas's booted foot, holding him in place.

"Don't just stand there, help us," one of the men said.

"Please," whimpered the other man that was on the floor.

"Serves you right," Lois said.

"She's right. You robbed us at gunpoint, and for what, a map?"

Lois looked at Caroline and swallowed hard, hoping that she hadn't seen her, but then Lois said, "This is a new one."

"She's with me," I said.

"That explains it. I better get the sheriff," she said, racing out the door.

Caroline shrugged and disappeared, as did Douglas. Within minutes, the sheriff ran into the room, with Andrew and Badass Bart right behind him, Lois making her way into the library last. The robbers raced toward the sheriff, and were quickly restrained by two other men who joined us in the library. "Oh, thank God. I thought we were goners for sure," one man said.

"Please, I'd rather be in jail than in here with that man!" one of them said.

The sheriff took a quick look around the room. "What man?"

"The one with the jagged knife. He held it to my throat, see?" the man said, raising his head a notch.

"Sorry, but I don't see anything wrong with your throat or any man in here besides Andrew and Badass Bart. They were with me searching the hotel for you."

"Those ladies saw him," he went on to say.

"What are they talking about, Agnes?" Lois asked.

"I have no idea. I think these men might just be mental."

The men were put into handcuffs, still insisting that a man with a jagged blade had threatened them. Once they were hauled from the room with the help of Badass Bart, laughter filled the room in a booming voice.

"Don't be concerned, Andrew. That's just Douglas, or as he's known, The Cutter."

Andrew's face whitened and he promptly escorted Lois and me from the room. I did a happy dance since I had my purse back. It was good to know that one of the ghosts that resided in the hotel had looked out for us tonight.

Eleanor ran toward me, giving me quite the hug. "Oh, Agnes. What an awful thing to go through, being robbed at gunpoint."

I smiled now, gasping since Eleanor was cutting off my air. "Eleanor, I can't breathe."

She let me go and shook her head, dabbing at a tear in her eye. "Agnes, don't scare me like that again. My ticker can't take it," she said, pounding her chest with a fist. "If anything ever happened to you I …I … I just don't know what I'd do."

"Not to worry, but I'd really like to head off to bed now."

"Just as soon as you tell me what really happened in that library," the sheriff said as he joined us.

"I don't know, really. I mean, the men were quite distraught when Lois and I walked into the library and they had some wild story about a man holding a knife to their throats. I feel a whole lot better knowing that they'll be put behind bars."

"Not so sure about bars since you managed to remove a few, but I'll lock them in cold storage until the U.S. Marshal can pick them up—hopefully, tomorrow sometime."

"How worried are you that these men were looking for a treasure map?"

He hooked his fingers in the loops of his pants. "Did they mention treasure or just a map?"

"Map, but I suspect that they were talking about a map to Leister's gold."

"We don't know that quite yet, but the problem is that the legend of those gold bars seems to be growing. I really need to speak to Francine about telling folks about the legend. The last thing I need to worry about is would-be treasure hunters."

Mr. Wilson pushed his walker forward. "Where did everyone go, and who are those fellas who were escorted out of here and over to the jailhouse? I sure hope that my sweet Eleanor hasn't gotten herself into any more trouble."

"Not me—Agnes. She was robbed at gunpoint."

"Sounds like her usual MO. How about we head upstairs now? I'm late for my night-time meds."

We made it into the elevator and I leaned my exhausted head on Andrew's shoulder. I just knew that when my head hit the pillow tonight that I'd be out like a light and that's just what happened not ten minutes later.

Chapter Twelve

When the sun rose early the next morning, I buried my head under my pillow. Our room faced the east and I could barely tolerate the harsh light that blasted through the thin curtains.

"I'll meet you downstairs for breakfast," Andrew said, leaving the room.

Once I was alone, I tried to formulate a plan of action. I'd sure like to see what Francine had to say about what happened last night. At least Lois seemed to be decent for the most part, but I wondered if she really wasn't able to open the register, or was trained to not open it, even if being robbed. Not that it made much sense, since we could have lost our lives if the robbers had gotten antsy about it.

Since the bright sun just wouldn't quit bothering me, I got up, made my way to the bathroom with my supplies and took a quick bath. As I rested back against the bathtub, all I could think about was how I missed modern things like television, cellular service, and a shower!

Today, I donned denim shorts and a white tee since I hoped we'd be able to explore the town a little more, with the cemetery as my first destination. I couldn't wait to find out how old the tombstones were, or see if I could find any interesting names among them.

After I put my things away, Eleanor greeted me on my way out of the room. "Hello, there. The men are already downstairs."

"I sure hope we won't miss breakfast. I'm starving."

We sauntered our way to the elevator, and once we were on our way down to the first floor, I couldn't help but wonder—. "Hey, Eleanor. Have you ever wondered what would happen if we pushed the M button? I mean, would it actually take us down to the mine shafts that run under the hotel?"

"Beats me, but maybe we shouldn't do that. I doubt it would work anyway, and I'd hate to miss another meal."

Drat, but I really wanted to try it at least once. "But what if the missing family is down there trapped? We could really save the day here."

"Is that what you want to do? Save the family just so you can get more recognition?"

"No, that's not what I meant. I was just making a joke, is all. You're right; we'll try it another time, perhaps later. After breakfast."

When the elevator came to a halt with jerk and screech of gears, Eleanor and I waltzed toward the dining room, joining Andrew and Mr. Wilson, but once again, they weren't alone. Mrs. Barry and the bird sisters were also there, and it appeared that Mrs. Barry was already a bit tipsy and it was only ten o'clock.

"Heello," Mrs. Barry slurred. "About time you girls got here."

I smiled kindly as Bonnie came over with her pot of coffee, pouring us a cup. "Bring another cup for Mrs. Barry, please," I said.

"I already have a cup," Mrs. Barry grinned.

"Oh, I know, but you need a cup without any of your sauce. It's much too early to be drinking anything other than straight, black coffee."

"Don't judge me," Mrs. Barry complained as she pounded a fist on the table, rattling the dishes. "As it so happens, I haven't been to bed yet."

"What?" I exclaimed. "That is so unhealthy."

Mrs. Peacock and Mrs. Canary helped Mrs. Barry up, apologizing. "She means no harm," Mrs. Peacock said. "I'll make sure she heads straight to bed."

"I'm not judging her, either, just so you know. Believe me, I like Mrs. Barry. She has spunk, and that's a great quality to have for the older generation."

"I'll sleep it off, I pr-promise," Mrs. Barry slurred. "I'd love to join you and Eleanor later for a tour of the Lemon Pine Mine, like at four."

"We'd be happy to do that, Mrs. Barry. Go on up to your room and get some sleep."

Mrs. Barry wobbled her way out of the dining room and I really hoped that she'd go straight to her room, although 'straight' and Mrs. Barry certainly didn't go hand in hand. Sure, she was a bit crotchety at times, but I'd always thought that, for the most part, it was all a deliberate act. Why, when Eleanor and I went to Redwater, Mrs. Barry always insisted that we stay with her. Yes, she had a certain charm about her.

Eleanor sipped her coffee, giving Mr. Wilson a once-over. He was once again dressed in black, and I had to admit that I liked his new look since he usually only wore gray workpants and shirts he most likely had worn since his working days.

"That Mrs. Peacock seemed a little sweet on you, Wilson," Eleanor said. "Don't think I didn't notice the way she batted her eyelashes at you when we walked up.

"It's not my fault that Mrs. Peacock knows a good thing when she sees one." He whistled as he spoke.

"Oh, is that right now? You're not the only one who can say that. Plenty of men find me attractive, you know."

"I wasn't saying they don't, but Frank Alton isn't here right now. It's quite a shame the way you flirt with him, since he's a married man."

"Why are you throwing Frank's name up right now? I haven't flirted with the man since you and I became serious. We're engaged, remember?"

"Seems like you've been dragging your feet over that, Eleanor," Mr. Wilson said with a shake of his head. "And if the truth be known, I'm tired of it."

"Calm down, Wilson," Andrew said. "You're not alone there. I'm in the same boat with Agnes. Perhaps if these two weren't so consumed with solving mysteries, we might just have a double wedding."

I gulped. "What?"

"How about it, Agnes? Let's set a date and get on with it."

I was saved from answering for the moment because my food was set in front of me. I immediately started shoveling in my bacon and eggs, casting a wary glance Andrew's way.

"Just as I figured," he said. "Come on, Wilson. Let's see if Patty is dealing today."

"Th-Thought you told me not to play cards in the saloon anymore."

"I know, but I feel a lucky streak coming on," Andrew said, as he left the table with Wilson trailing after him with his walker.

I sighed. "Great, all I need now is for Andrew to start pressuring me to set a date."

"We've been engaged for a while now. Maybe it's time to set a date. They didn't say it had to be soon, now, did they?" Eleanor laughed.

"True that."

Eleanor and I finished our breakfast in relative silence and I really hoped that Andrew wouldn't be too mad at me. I did love him, but at my age, I had no intention of being rushed to the altar—and none of that was worth worrying about since I already had enough on my plate with the investigation that seemed to be going nowhere at the moment.

GHOSTLY HIJINKS

I stood and stretched for a moment, waiting for Eleanor to stand, too. "Let's check out that elevator. I want to at least try to go down to the mine," I whispered so nobody would overhear me.

"Oh, I'm not so sure that's a good idea. The Lemon Pine Mine might be an even better place to start our search."

"I don't see any reason that we can't check both places, Eleanor."

"Fine, but I don't like it, I'll tell you that. I can't help feel that something bad will come of it."

"What are you talking about? What could possibly go wrong?"

We strolled back to the elevator and waved at Lois, who actually smiled back at me. I guess after our ordeal yesterday that Lois had made an about-face, which was great in my book since I hated feeling out of sorts with anyone.

Once we were in the elevator and the doors closed, I poised to push the M button. "Think, Agnes. Are you sure we should do this?"

"Why are you such a worrywart?"

"Well, we have no idea just how deep the mine is or how sturdy the elevator is. We could plummet all the way down and be killed."

"I suppose, but I feel like today is our lucky day, too. Why should Andrew be the only one with the luck?"

I pushed the button and waited with bated breath for something, anything, to happen, but when it didn't, I shrugged. "I guess it doesn't work."

The lights in the elevator flashed and I felt chilled to my bone. "Oh, Caroline," I called her. "Wherever are you?"

Caroline appeared and shook her finger at me. "Shame on you, Agnes. You shouldn't have pushed that button."

The lights quit flashing and I smiled. "See, nothing bad happened, Eleanor."

Before Eleanor answered, the elevator soared to the third floor at a fast rate, dinged, and then raced downward. By now, our screams echoed in the small elevator and Eleanor and I had our arms wrapped around one another, holding onto each other for dear life. When the elevator came to a sudden halt, it was between the first and second floors.

"Lucky day, eh?" Eleanor asked. "Some luck this is."

I wiggled out of Eleanor's arms and pushed the emergency button, clamping my palms over my sensitive ears as a loud alarm went off. A voice then came on and said, "How can I help you?" in a foreign accent.

"We're stuck in the elevator," I said.

"What city are you from?"

"Silver, Nevada. You mean you're not from the Goldberg Hotel?"

"Oh, no. This is a call center in India."

"You can't be serious here!" I choked out. "How in the heck is an operator from India gonna help us out of this blasted elevator?"

"Calm down. I'll alert the management right away. Where did you say you were again?"

"The Goldberg Hotel in Silver, Nevada, USA."

"It might be easier if I get someone to help," Caroline suggested.

"How, when you're not supposed to let anyone see you?"

"You told me she let Lois see her yesterday," Eleanor pointed out.

"I didn't mean to. I guess in all the excitement, I let my guard down. I promise I won't let it happen again, but maybe I should fetch someone here."

I was about to tell Caroline to not even think about doing that, but just then I heard a knocking on the elevator door and it was wrenched open, with Redd staring down at us from the floor above. "I should have known. Take it easy, ladies. I'll have you out just as soon as I can."

Caroline was still here and I tried to shoo her off, but she whispered in my ear with, "I promise, I won't leave you."

"No, I think it would be better if you disappear now."

"You're so fickle, Agnes, but your wish is my command." She faded away and I felt bad that I had to ask her to leave, but I just couldn't risk someone else seeing her.

Eleanor folded her arms across her ample chest. "This is such a good 'I told you so' moment, but I'm not going to do it. I'm not going to tell you I told you this wasn't a good idea and that I had a bad feeling about it. I so won't tell you Agnes, I really won't, but I'll be thinking it. I'll be thinking about it really hard," she said, pointing to her noggin.

"Oh, thanks. What a pal you are. I'm so glad you won't tell me you told me so, or rub it in my face," I smirked. "You know, like the going inside a jail cell."

Eleanor chuckled. "I'll have to admit that wasn't one of my brighter moments. I just hope we're not stuck in here, *all day*. Not with that sensitive bladder of yours."

"Eleanor, why did you have to even go there? Now I hafta pee!"

"You can hold it. I have confidence in you and your nervous bladder." She winked.

"Do you think you ladies could climb out if I helped you?"

"Are you nuts? We're too old to do that," I said.

"Yeah, us old women aren't that agile," Eleanor added.

I smiled at that, since Eleanor liked to deny that we were of a certain age, or weren't capable of doing things like the younger folks could. Sometimes, even I was surprised with how my body could move when it had the proper inspiration—like if someone chased me with a gun. Sure, my hip might hurt at times, but all of that gets thrown to the wayside when I'm up to my neck in trouble.

Redd disappeared, and I hoped that he was fixing the blasted elevator since I now had to cross my legs. I fell headlong into Eleanor when the elevator jerked into motion, and now all I could think about was being hurtled down to the mineshaft, and who knew how far down that would be.

I was relieved when the elevator stopped on the first floor and we wobbled out. Lois was right at hand, asking, "Are you ladies okay?"

I couldn't answer, as I was making a beeline toward the ladies' room. "She has to pee," I overheard Eleanor explain.

Redd was waiting for me when I came out of the bathroom with a question-ready-to-ask look on his face. "So, what happened in there? I've never known the elevator to act like that unless the M button was pushed."

"Oh? Well, we were just going up to our room after breakfast," I lied.

"Yes, and that elevator just went nuts," Eleanor added somberly. "Are you sure that elevator is safe?"

"Sure it is, but I suppose I'll use it a few times to make sure it's up to working standards."

"What if you get stuck in there?" I asked. "I'm pretty positive those fellas from the India call center won't be able to help you."

"The what?"

"When we used that emergency phone, some fella from India answered. Wouldn't it be way easier if it just went to the front desk?"

"I'll have to ask Francine about that. I wasn't aware it did."

I narrowed my eyes slightly. "How don't you know? I thought you were the main maintenance man around here?"

"I believe I told you I do more than just that, like wherever I'm needed. I'm glad you ladies are doing okay. I really had better check out the elevator now."

After Redd went into the elevator, I strode in the direction of the swinging front door. "Shouldn't we check on Andrew and Mr. Wilson?" Eleanor asked.

"You can if you want, but I want to check out the cemetery, if you don't mind."

GHOSTLY HIJINKS

"Okay, but Mr. Wilson seemed mad and he never gets mad. What if he's fed up with me?" Eleanor sniffled now, dabbing at the corner of her eye with her shirt. "Mrs. Peacock might be real competition. She's so sophisticated."

"I'm sure he'll be just fine after he does his male bonding with Andrew. Mrs. Peacock is from Redwater, not East Tawas, so I don't believe she's a threat. Besides, you're just as sophisticated as she is. You're both from small towns in Michigan."

"Th-That's true, but she has a Macaw that can talk and—"

"Cuss," I finished for her. "If it's a pet you want, you should get one."

"Like a dog?"

"Those take quite a bit of work, Eleanor. I was thinking more on the lines of a cat."

"I don't much like the idea of that. I'd hate to clean a litterbox."

"How about a fish, then?"

"Maybe I really don't need a pet. I can barely take care of myself."

"You said it, Eleanor, not me." I tried hard not to smile since Eleanor was really being candid right now.

I noticed as I crossed the street that dirt was placed over the entire street and I wondered what else I'd have to expect from the festival—hopefully not another law breaker. Being robbed at gunpoint sure wasn't my fondest memory of Silver. I thought Douglas and his interest in Eleanor was. I sure hoped Mr. Wilson never learned of it. I'd hate to see the ghost injure poor Mr. Wilson, but then again he could be a tad spunky at times.

We waltzed past Jo Ellen's bed and breakfast, the only brick building in town where a woman wearing an apron over her dress was sweeping off the steps. We gave her a wave as she glanced up, but continued along the street since the clapboard sidewalk ended on the other side of the jail. It seemed odd how the jailhouse was right next door to a bed and breakfast. Might even be a good place to ask a few questions. I really would love to hear the story about Leister's gold from more people. I kept hoping that I'd run into someone who knew more than what we'd been told so far.

I felt the heat bearing down on us from the sun now and felt sweat creep down my back as we passed the bank. Next, there was a blank space between the bank and cemetery, but there were bricks embedded into the ground, which I figured might just have been a building of some sort at one time. The livery stable was across the street from the bank with a decent-sized corral full of horses.

"Wow, I wonder why so many horses?" I mused aloud.

"I saw horse trailers hauling into town last night," Eleanor said. "They must have some more activities that involve horses later. I heard talk of a stampede coming through town later."

"These folks sure do a festival up right."

Cars and trucks passed us by, many of them packed with gear of some sort, all heading out of town, though. The cemetery had an iron fence that went around it, although from where we were, it didn't look all that big with the doors wide open. Next to that was a small building with a man outside working with wood.

"Look, he's building coffins," Eleanor pointed out.

I gulped. "I sure hope that's for the festival. You know, to give it more of the western flavor."

I heard what sounded like a shovel striking the ground and I entered the cemetery slowly, wondering what else the townspeople could be up to. It sure didn't seem like they'd be digging a grave for the festival. I imaged the bodies of outlaws out on display in those coffins that we'd walked by.

"Hurry up, Clark. The last thing we need is for anyone to see what we're up to."

"It would help, Gertie, if you ... I don't know ... maybe picked up a shovel to help me? My back is aching already."

Eleanor and I hid behind a worn tombstone, or tried to since it was way smaller than us, but the couple we spied didn't seem to notice us. I bit my fist when I saw what they were doing and I just couldn't stop myself from going over there, but before I made my move, Eleanor whispered in my ear, "I'm going for the sheriff."

Caroline, I really need you right now, I thought, hoping that she'd appear from whereever it was that she hung out. She popped in right next to me and I clapped my hands over my mouth before I made a noise, since she'd scared the bejeezus out of me. I gave her a look, but that's as far as it went since I now boldly strutted over to where they were digging. Clark was in a hole with his shovel now and that made me so mad. Why … these two were grave robbers.

"What are you doing?" I asked in what I thought was my most intimidating voice.

Clark stopped, mid-shovel, and glared at me. "Find yourself another grave, this one is mine."

"What on earth are you doing that for? It's not only against the law, but really morbid."

Gertie rolled her eyes, wiping back a strand of her blonde hair. "What's it to you, old bat? Shouldn't you be home knitting or something?" She laughed with a snort.

I balled up my fist, but Caroline held a hand against my chest, preventing me from getting too physical like I really wanted to do. Good thing, since I wasn't like that, but grave-robbing sure fired up my kettle.

The shovel hit the ground and I said in a much louder voice, "Stop doing that now!"

"Who's going to stop us, Grandma?"

"I am," Sheriff Bradley said from behind me. "Drop the shovel, now."

The shovel was dropped and Clark crawled out of the grave, brushing off his clothing.

"We're not doing anything wrong," Gertie spat. "There's not even a body in that grave."

"And no gold bars, either," Clark grumbled. "I was sure this was the place to look."

"Leister's gold again?" The sheriff palmed his head. "When will you folks figure out that Leister's gold is just a story to tell the tourists? There's no gold hidden anywhere hereabouts."

"That's what you say, but we know better. My grand-pappy told me all about how Peyton Leister melted that gold down into bars and hid it right here in Silver."

"That seems strange. If the folks of Silver gave Peyton that bad of a time, why on Earth would he hide the gold here, of all places?" I asked.

Caroline smiled, gave Clark a kick and he flew back into the hole he'd dug with a thump. He jumped back up and clamored out, shouting, "Why did you push me?"

"Nobody pushed you, unless it was perhaps Peyton Leister's ghost," I suggested.

"That's not funny. There's no such thing as ghosts."

"No?" I cocked a brow at Caroline, who threw her arms out and went into a spin, scattering dust into a cloud that chased Clark and Gertie out of the cemetery.

"And don't come back," the sheriff hollered.

"Is that all you're gonna do?" I asked.

"Pretty much. Do you know how many times that grave has been dug up? Too many to count, I tell you." The sheriff smiled now. "I assure you this bothers me, but I just can't arrest everyone who acts out of the norm during the festival. The marshal just picked up the robbers earlier."

"That's good to hear since they did rob me at gunpoint. So what are your plans today in the way of securing the graveyard?"

"Not much I can do unless you ladies want to guard it. I sure hope a dust storm isn't brewing with that little whirlwind that just blew through here, but I suspect someone will be back here before the day is over."

GHOSTLY HIJINKS

"When the sheriff walked away, I asked, "But what about that hole?"

"It can stay empty. If I put the dirt back in the hole, some fool will just dig it back up later."

"Why doesn't that grave have a body in it?"

"Look, Agnes. I'm not even sure if that grave *ever* had a body in it, if it was already looted, or even moved." He didn't stick around to answer any more of my questions.

I frowned, but there wasn't too much I could do. I sure hoped that I wouldn't run into Clark and Gertie again anytime soon. Who knew if they were desperate types?

"Gertie is a strange name for a young woman these days."

"Unless someone really didn't like their baby," Eleanor agreed. "I don't even like my name. There are so many Eleanor's of our generation."

Eleanor had me by ten years, but I didn't say so. She never cared all that much to be reminded of that fact.

I walked toward the tombstone with the name, Peyton Leister, on it. "I wonder if Peyton was ever buried here."

"For all we know, someone had just put the tombstone here. Since Leister's gold is such a big legend around Silver, it seems fitting that he have some sort of a resting place."

"That's just it; I fully intend to speak with Francine about this. She has to know something more than she's telling me."

"Fine, but I'm not sure how much we'll learn from her. If she's already tight-lipped about the details of the gold bars, what makes you think that she'll tell us where Peyton Leister's body really is?"

"She might not, but who else can we ask?"

"I'm not sure, but someone has to know."

I sighed, feeling more frustrated than I ever had before. Something just had to give, and sooner rather than later, before all was lost.

Chapter Thirteen

Not long after we left the cemetery, I came back to the hotel to ask Andrew for the key fob, even though I really wanted to distance myself from him right now. I vowed that today I just had to press on and find the family before it was too late. We'd lost sight of Caroline after she chased Clark and Gertie from the cemetery, which had to have been the most entertaining thing I'd ever witnessed. The strange thing was the sheriff seemed to think it was only a whirlwind when it was far from it. It didn't seem like anything really rattled the sheriff. He reminded me of my granddaughter's husband, Trooper Bill Sales.

As it turned out, we didn't have to go out to Francine's house since she was behind the counter when we walked in. We greeted her with a smile, and I asked, "Where is Lois?"

"Using the bathroom. What's up?"

"Oh, do I look like something is up?"

"Seems to be your MO, so why not just spill it? I have things to attend to today out at the mining camp."

"Mining camp?"

"Yes, tourists like to pitch tents a few miles out of town during the festival. It's a half-mile from the Lemon Pine Mine."

My face lit up. "Really? We're planning to head out to the mine later for a tour. When our friend sleeps it off. She did a little too much celebrating last night."

"I think I know the one you're talking about. Just whatever you

149

do, please stay with the tour group. If you get lost in those mining shafts, we'll probably never see you again."

Was that actually genuine concern like it sounded, or was that some kind of ploy to keep us from investigating? "I'll take that under consideration."

"She means we won't," Eleanor said. "What we really wanted to know was about Peyton Leister's grave. Was he ever buried in that cemetery?"

I examined Francine's face intently. "Probably not, but I can't be sure since that was way before my time, you understand."

"Point taken, but someone must have thought his grave was worthy enough to be dug up, but the sheriff wasn't even concerned."

"It's commonplace around here during the festival."

"Perhaps it wouldn't be if you quit telling folks that story about Peyton."

"It's much too late for that now. Tourists really love that story and it makes for a much better festival. I can't even image not mentioning it."

"It's your business, of course, but I hope you realize that you're responsible for at least one family's death, the Thompsons. Anyone who follows that story and goes out on their own looking for that treasure is a direct connection to you, Francine."

"I'd hate to have that on my conscience," Eleanor added.

"I guess this is where we differ, or should just agree to disagree. I'm in no way responsible for anyone going off half-cocked and looking for the legendary treasure."

I smiled stiffly and had to walk away from her now, before I said something really bad, like she was guilty of being indirectly responsible for that first family's deaths. If only I were able to learn the details of their deaths. Finding their bodies in the desert just seemed too convenient.

Once we were back outside, Eleanor asked, "What now?"

GHOSTLY HIJINKS

"We're going to ask a few more questions, like at that bed and breakfast."

When we made our way across the street and into the brick building that housed Jo Ellen's Bed and Breakfast, it was bustling with activity. The main desk had a woman around our age sitting in an office chair and I guessed she was checking guests in from the way she was passing forms for them to fill out and handing each a key with a kind smile.

I stared around at the wallpaper-covered walls that were beige with green stripes. That took me back to my great-grandmother's house, which was similarly decorated. Guests were milling around and I asked a man near us what they were waiting for.

"We're going out to the Lemon Pine Mine today. Jo Ellen has set us up with a special tour, promising to give a few tips about the history of Leister's gold. It's said that it's only a legend back in Reno, but I can see it's alive and well here in Silver. It's why we made the trip here during the festival," he whispered. "I've even heard they'll allow us to do a little digging in the mine."

I smiled. "Oh, really? I didn't know that. When does it start?"

"Already was supposed to have started, but I guess Jo Ellen's still too busy checking in the guests. We're the only ones allowed on the tour, you know. I booked my room two years ago."

"M-Me too," I said with a shrug.

Jo Ellen stood up and stretched. "Okay, folks, I suppose we should get going now. I'll check the rest of you in when we get back."

"Isn't it about lunch now?" a woman said, clutching her belly.

"Sure is, but we've packed picnic baskets full of goodies and will be eating it just as soon as we get there. Now remember, I expect each and every one of you to stay tight-lipped about my little tour from the rest of the tourists here in town. The man running the tour at the mine has given us permission to go deeper into the mine, but that doesn't mean that it's completely safe. Wendy is handing out waivers that you'll all need to sign before we leave."

We quickly signed our waivers and my heart beat hard now. I just hoped no one asked our names or discovered that we didn't fit in with this group. Eleanor was quite the actress, but even she was playing low key now.

Once everyone had signed the paperwork, we were led outside where a bus awaited us. As we boarded, I notice the last three seats were missing and supplies were stored back there, like hand-held pickaxes. All I could think about was just how dangerous that might be. Anyone could harm themselves with them, and if need be, I'd voice my opinion once I figured out what they were really up to.

Once everyone boarded, the bus moved out and we headed out of town, the group talking excitedly. "If I find the gold bars, I'm going to move to Paris, France," one vivacious young lady said.

Snickers were heard, and the man ahead of us said, "Paris, France? What on earth for?"

"Because I'm sick of the ole U-S-of-A is why. I crave culture and a French boyfriend."

"You think that now, but you can't even speak French, can you?"

"Pierre will teach me."

"Who is Pierre?"

"The French boyfriend that I'll find, duh," the young lady went on to say.

"You won't find any gold, Marsha, because I'm going to find it all and I'm not sharing with anyone," a young man said.

"Carson, you're really out of your mind if you think that."

"How about you white folks just take it down a notch," another woman said. "That gold has Unique's name all over it. Isn't that right, Ramone?" she asked the man accompanying her.

"That's right, baby."

"Calm down, folks," Jo Ellen said. "We're not going to find Leister's gold in the mine."

"Well, where are we gonna find it, then?" Marsha asked, leaning forward in her seat. "You said on your brochure that—"

GHOSTLY HIJINKS

"I never said you'd find Leister's gold, just that I'd take you in the mine where you might find a few gold nuggets, is all."

"We'll explain everything to you once we're in the mine," a woman sitting next to Jo Ellen said.

"Wendy is right. Just be patient until then."

Fifteen minutes later, the bus rumbled up a drive that had a sign in big, white letters that read, Lemon Pine Mine. The bus parked and we unloaded, and for once, the group was quiet as church mice.

Jo Ellen gathered everyone together as an old, slender man strode forward. "Howdy, folks. My names Big Jake and I'll be your tour guide today."

Great, another man with a nickname. But I listened intently as he told us his rules. "Rule number one: stay with the group. Rule number two: don't dig anywhere unless we tell you it's okay unless you want to fill the mine shafts with water and drown everyone."

"Water?" I asked.

"Yes, ma'am. It's almost happened a few times now. There's an underground spring that was found to run along the side of the north mineshaft, and in 1910 it was tapped into, sorta the reason we found it in the first place. Anyway, it flooded the mineshaft and twenty men drowned. The mine had to be pumped out and that section of the shaft is now off limits. As a safeguard, we don't ever allow anyone too close to the north shaft. They abandoned that section of the mine after the accident."

"So there might just be gold over there, then?" Unique asked.

"That's not what I said. I said it's not safe over there," Big Jake said with a stern look. "Let's just say this, when the spring was tapped into, the water rushed in so fast that the miners never stood a chance."

Unique gulped and clammed up finally, as we were led inside. The main entrance was smaller than I expected and some of the taller ones had to stoop down to get in, but once we were inside, the main area was more open. "This area was opened more for tours. As you can see, there are timbers on the walls and ceilings of the mines to keep the soft dirt from caving in. It's constantly building pressure and new timbers were also added to the existing ones to keep the mine from collapsing. All the timbers above your heads are original and have done quite a good job of holding up the ceiling of the mine. You'll find them all along the shafts. I'd be careful and not run into any of the timbers on the side. I can't assure just how safe it will remain."

"What's that pipe near the ceiling?" Marsha asked.

"That's for ventilation. Otherwise, it can get a might dusty down here." He went on to explain, "The shaft we'll be going in is uncharted for anyone other than Jo Ellen's guests, so consider yourselves fortunate."

I raised my hand, and when he pointed to me, I asked, "Has anyone ever ventured into the shafts without you knowing about it?"

"We keep a pretty good watch on our tour groups here."

"I'm sure you do, but what about after hours?"

"Never has happened that I know of. Only a fool would attempt such a thing at night. The mineshafts go on for miles and even I can get a little confused at times. That's why even I only go in only so deep."

I had a few more questions, but didn't want to voice them. I'd wait until the tour was over before I questioned Big Jake further. Wendy brought in the picnic baskets. We munched on sandwiches and were each given a bottle of water as we listened to Jo Ellen talk about Peyton Leister.

"Silver was founded in 1850 and, once gold was found, the town quickly was built as folks came to town once they got word."

"Is it true that there was a Winfield Hotel here once that burned to the ground, the same site where the Goldberg Hotel & Saloon now is?" I asked.

GHOSTLY HIJINKS

Jo Ellen's brow furrowed. "And who told you about that? It's not common knowledge."

We heard it at the Willington General Store."

"Did Glenda also tell you that it was a mining dispute and that arson was suspected? That the ground where the Goldberg sits now is cursed, some say, since they never even bothered looking for the bodies. Jessup Goldberg was one greedy man. It's no wonder he met an untimely end."

"So he knew about it and didn't care? Just built overtop of them?"

"Exactly what I'm saying. Dying from pneumonia was too good for the likes of him. They say he kept a woman locked up, a prostitute that he'd gotten pregnant. Rumor was that he killed her and the baby."

"I've heard that, too, but is there any truth to it?"

"You sure have a lot of questions." Jo Ellen said. "What are you, some kind of historian?"

"I consider myself a history buff, but just as a hobby."

"I see. Well, back to Peyton Leister. Nobody knows for sure what year he came to Silver, but he came in like a hotshot. He didn't reside with the other miners in tent city. He had himself a small cabin on the other side of town, far from the rest of the miners. Nobody even knows where he found his gold and he wasn't talking. What he did best was brag, but that didn't help him a bit when he found a huge amount of gold that nobody would let him turn in."

"That seems strange."

"Folks can go against you in a heartbeat. The thing is, you couldn't afford to make enemies back then. I suspect folks were a might jealous and wanted to know where he hid his stash. He stayed for days in that cabin of his and folks said you could see the smoke from his fire all the way into town. The sheriff went out there to check it out, but Peyton ran him off his claim. You could do that back then as long as you weren't breaking the law."

"After Peyton disappeared from town, folks found a kettle with gold in the bottom of it, and boards lying around in the shape of bars. They figured he had melted his gold into bars and taken it with him, right out of town, but days later when his wagon was found in the desert, the gold wasn't anywhere to be found."

"What about Peyton, did they him dead?"

"Not from what I heard, but I suspect he died of exposure after he was stranded when his wagon wheel had broken off. When there weren't any deep wheel tracks in the dirt, folks assumed he didn't have the gold with him, that he had hidden it for safekeeping until he returned. Some suspected that it was too much gold to haul off by himself and that he was off to report to the U.S. Marshal about the corruption in Silver since he wasn't able to sell his gold."

"That sounds like a good reason to murder a man," I said.

"But they say his body was never found."

"No? Then why is there a tombstone with his name on it?"

"I can't say, ma'am. Word is that his body was never found. I suppose they must have wanted to give the man some kind of resting place."

"That must be it because his remains certainly aren't at the cemetery since there were grave robbers there this morning. Aren't you a little curious if Peyton was murdered?"

"Not really. His story has turned into a legend that sure is interesting, but today we're not here looking for Leister's gold. Nobody has ever turned it up in all these years, and, believe me, plenty have looked. Problem is that not many came back alive, they just left one day to look for the treasure and never came back."

"Like the Thompsons," I said.

"Who told you about them? That's unfortunate, but their car broke down in the desert and they didn't have any survival skills. If they had stayed with their car they might have survived, but their bodies were found about a mile away in the desert. It's not very smart to go anywhere down Highway 50 without making sure that you have both food and water."

"So you don't suspect foul play?"

"Why would I?"

I couldn't hold myself back now. "It's just that I wondered if the Thompsons were searching for Leister's gold. You know, like the family that disappeared from the Goldberg not long ago."

"Not sure of when that might have happened."

"Really, in a small town such as this? It seems like you'd keep up to date about a big thing like a second missing family, especially tourists."

"Not really sure where you're going here, but I'd like to mosey into the mine shaft now and give you folks a chance to find a gold nugget or two."

"It's about time," Unique sighed. "I swear I never knew old folks could yap so much."

"Of course in my days, younger folks were taught to respect their elders," Big Jake said. "Anyone wanting to know an in-depth history of Silver is okay in my book. It seems like younger folks don't even care about things like that anymore."

I smiled as we were each handed a helmet with a light attached, just like you'd see in one of those adventures where tourists get trapped in an abandoned mine or underground cavern. We then headed up a long shaft that came to a fork with one to the right and the other to the left. "Take the one to the left," Big Jake said.

When I passed the one on the right, I couldn't help but sneak a peek inside, but it was too dark to see much of anything. I wanted to go down there, if only I had the chance. Small pickaxes were handed out when we were in a different mine shaft and Big Jake demonstrated how we should pick along one area only. We were also told that we could keep what we found, which brought a smile to Eleanor's face.

Unique and Ramone strode farther ahead until Big Jake said, "Stay right here. I don't want you getting lost in the mineshaft."

I took that moment to slip away, tugging Eleanor along with me, unseen by Big Jake, Jo Ellen, and Wendy who were helping the other guests on their technique as they picked, looking for a morsel of gold.

Once we were out of sight, Eleanor asked, "Where are we going?"

"I'd like to check out the other shaft, is all."

"Th-That doesn't sound safe at all. You heard what Big Jake said."

"We'll be fine, and won't go in that far. I promise. If we don't see anything of interest, we'll just come on back out and re-join the group."

"Why is it that I feel so uneasy about this?"

"Quit being a worrywart."

"I can't help it. Maybe you should call Caroline to join us. I think I'd feel more comfortable having her here. After the way she handled those grave robbers, I have a new appreciation for having her on our team."

Giggling could be heard from behind Eleanor and she whirled to see Caroline standing behind her. "Thanks, Eleanor. I like you, too."

There were rocks all along the shaft and the wooden beams didn't look quite as sturdy as in the other parts of the mine. "I bet this was the shaft that was flooded. We'd better be extra careful."

"Which will only work if we leave right now," Eleanor said. "Agnes, it is too dangerous to be in here."

"I just want to see if the family is lost in here." I froze when after a few feet, there was a body on the floor in a sitting position against the wall of the mine.

"Oh, oh. I told you this was a bad idea. We just found another body."

I heard a crunching of stones behind us and Big Jake stepped forward. "You'll find plenty of bodies if you were to travel the length of the mine, but how about we not add you ladies to the list. Come along now, this area of the mine just isn't safe."

GHOSTLY HIJINKS

I stared at the beam overhead and loose stones were covering us with dust as they trickled from the ceiling. I hurried along with my arm looped through Eleanor's arm to make sure that she came along with me. Caroline bobbed silently next to us and didn't disappear until we were back in the main part of the mine.

"So what are you really here for?"

"I just wanted to take a quick look. There's a missing family I had hoped to locate. Trisha, Aaron and their daughter, Rebecca Jameson, disappeared from the Goldberg Hotel in the middle of the night."

"I heard that, but I assure you they never came this way. Francine called me and I checked the mine, but there was no sign of them. Maybe those folks went home."

"Do you believe in strange occurrences or the paranormal?"

"I sure do. This mine is haunted by many spirits, believe me, if that's what you mean."

"Actually, no. I had a dream and I just know that the family is in trouble." I went on to tell him all about my dream and how some of the details had proven to be true—like Francine and Sheriff Wilford, the actor.

"If you think they went after Leister's gold, they wouldn't come here. What you folks need to do is look for Peyton's cabin. It was located on the opposite side of town about a mile away. Peyton never mined here."

"Have you ever been there?"

"On occasion, but none of my searches ever turned up any gold. My firm belief is that the story has been modified as it was told. There might never have been any gold and I do wish that Peyton's story wasn't so glamorized, but it does bring in the tourists."

"Thanks, Big Jake, we'll check that out."

"Just don't do it alone and be sure you have plenty of water. I'd even tell you to bring the sheriff with you just in case someone is checking out the same area. Especially with the festival going on right now."

"The thing is that we're stuck here now, until the group is done."

"That's just fine. Come on back and see what you can find. You just might end up with a nugget."

We passed a small machine and I had to ask, "What's that for?"

"That's from the 1876 invention, the wiggle-tail, or widow-maker as it's been nicknamed, because when that machine runs, it creates quite a bit of dust. Many miners died from being exposed to that dust."

"That seems like it wouldn't be such a great thing to use, then."

"Yes, but they used it for striking into the rock, so it really served a purpose and it was much easier than doing it by hand. There was plenty of ore in this area of the mine."

"But they did find gold, too, right?"

"Sure did, ma'am, in the area where we're allowing you to check. Now, let's get back to the others."

When we went back to where the rest of the group was picking at the walls, I could see that this was just for entertainment purposes since there was just no way that we'd ever find anything, but Eleanor really got into swinging her pick axe at the wall and with menacing intent, I must say.

"I have to use the bathroom," Unique said.

"There's a Porta Potty outside," Big Jake said. "I'll show you."

"No, no need. I can find it. Can't be too hard to find."

Ramone went along with her, and when they didn't come back in what seemed like a long time, I whispered to Eleanor, "I think those two are up to something."

I walked up the shaft and back down the other juncture. We walked for some time, even passing the body we had seen earlier. We continued into the shaft when we began to hear voices. I rushed forward, hoping that it was the missing family, but it was Unique and Ramone. While Unique held a long bar in her hands, Ramone struck the end of it with a large hammer. Boom ... boom ... boom! The racket was unmistakable.

GHOSTLY HIJINKS

"Stop it, you two!" I shouted above the noise they were making. "You heard what Big Jake told you about this shaft."

"Go on back to the group and mind your business, Grandma," Unique said. "The only reason he don't want us here is because there's gold over here, an untapped area."

I heard a rushing noise; my eyes widened and we backed up as a trickle of water began to seep out of the upper surface of the wall. "You've sprung a leak, you fool!" I shouted above the now roaring sound, racing as fast as I could up the mineshaft to alert the others. By the time I made it back into the main corridor, we were ankle deep in water. Eleanor and I met the rest of the group that ran in a panic for the entrance of the mine.

"What have you done?" Big Jake asked.

"It wasn't us, it was Unique and Ramone."

The water was getting deeper now, and we were wading toward the entrance, the water now to our knees, but a loud voice stopped us. "Help, Unique's trapped under a large rock," Ramone said.

"Get out, everyone. I'll help her," Big Jake said.

Ramone went back into the shaft with Big Jake and I followed, with Eleanor shouting, "Don't you dare, Agnes Barton."

I didn't listen, though, and continued to follow Big Jake and Ramone. Unique was struggling to keep her head above the water, and I helped hold her head up as Big Jake and Ramone lifted the large rock that had fallen, pinning Unique's ankle. It took a few tries before she was released and I helped Unique stand, but Big Jake moved in and picked up Unique like she weighed nothing. Moving up the shaft, the water was now at my thigh level and my hip ached as I waded for the entrance that loomed in the distance. It seemed like it was so far away, miles, but it wasn't quite as far as it seemed. After a minute or two, we finally made it outside.

"Keep moving," Big Jake said.

"Where's the bus?" I shrieked.

"Hopefully, they moved it to higher ground." Jake led the way to a set of stairs that ascended upward, and I huffed and puffed as I climbed them. Once we were up above the opening of the mine, I wanted to drop from exhaustion, but Big Jake said, "Keep moving."

When I glanced below, water was pouring out of the mouth of the mine. We walked quite a spell until Jake, exhausted, set Unique down, resting her back against a boulder. I sat down, too, wondering if Eleanor and the others made it to safety.

"Wh-What, now?" I asked.

"Hopefully, they've gone for help."

"So we're stuck on this mountain until then?"

"We can go down the other side, but the stones are quite loose. It might make a treacherous descent for you, ma'am."

"How am I going to get down? I can't even walk," Unique whined.

"Slide your big ass all the way down." Big Jake spat. "It told you how dangerous it was in the north shaft, but did you listen? No!"

"Calm down, Big Jake. There's nothing we can do about that now, but we need to get off this mountain or we'll bake for sure."

"True, but greenhorns really make me mad when they don't listen."

"Why can't they send a helicopter to save us?" Unique asked.

"Well, do you see any place they could land her, missy?"

"N-No, I don't."

"Okay, then. Let's move and get down off this mountain," Big Jake said.

Ramone helped Unique up and she hobbled on one foot until he carried her to the side where Big Jake told us that we'd be going down. Once there, I gave the steep slope a dirty look with all those tiny stones that would, for sure, send us flying to the bottom in a quick hurry if we weren't careful.

"Go down nose first, and kick your heels into the dirt of the slope to keep yourself from sliding all the way to the bottom. You have one good foot, girl, so you're gonna have to do the best you can. We'll keep you between us men so you can't fall to the bottom."

Tears streaked Unique's face and she nodded.

"Should I go first?" I asked.

"Nope, you go last. I don't want to see you falling to the bottom."

"That's great. Grandma is gonna get us all killed," Unique said.

"No, that would be you, dear."

Ramone went down first; his fingers clenched into a claw-like grip, his feet striking into the dirt as he slowly went down. I gulped hard, watching the technique and hoped when it was my turn I'd be able to do it. What I wanted to do was scream at the top of my lungs, "Go on without me." *Oh, Caroline. I really need you now.*

I went to my hands and knees when it was finally my turn and ground my feet into the dirt and stones, my fingers clawed into the dirt.

"Try to relax, Agnes. You're the bravest person I know," Caroline said as she hovered next to me.

I nodded. "I'll try."

As I moved down, stones were loosened and fell to the ground below. I heard Ramone holler, "I'm falling."

"Get a grip, man," Big Jake said. "Use your feet to catch yourself."

My muscles ached and I slid a few feet myself, but was able to catch myself. We seemed to all have our times of slipping more than we had intended, but after what seemed like hours, we were all at the bottom safety, lying on the ground in exhaustion.

The sun was in the west now and I dreaded being out here at night, with what would prove to be near freezing conditions. I lifted my head up when I heard a motor race toward us, and we all sat up, crying as we saw a Hummer come into view.

Sheriff Bradley jumped out of the passenger seat and ran toward us. "Are you folks all okay?"

"We are now," Big Jake said. "But this young lady is injured."

"H-How did you find us?" I asked.

"I know the area well enough to know if that mine ever flooded where the escape route was and just where Big Jake would come off the mountain."

Unique was carried by Big Jake and gently set in the Hummer, and once we were all safely inside, the vehicle sped toward town.

"Lucky for us, Jeff's brother was in town for the festival. You know—the actor. He didn't even hesitate to help out."

"So the rest of Jo Ellen's group made it safely into town?"

"Sure did, and that friend of yours, Eleanor, was quite beside herself. The others forced her to leave you behind since you were trying to help out that young lady there. Mighty brave of you."

"It sure was," Unique finally admitted. "You saved my life back there, Grandma. You're all right in my book."

"Actually, I think we can all say that Big Jake saved the day."

Everyone laughed, and when I looked over at Big Jake, he didn't look a bit smug about the attention everyone was giving. Humble to a fault.

Chapter Fourteen

When we finally got back to town, I asked to be dropped off at the Goldberg Hotel.

"You mean you weren't really part of Jo Ellen's group after all?" Big Jake asked.

"Nope. Sorry to deceive you all like that."

"Never really thought you were. You were a little too interested in the history of Silver and that missing family."

That didn't surprise me since I took it that Big Jake was wise beyond his years that looked plentiful from the lines that marred his face, and not in an unattractive way.

The Hummer skidded to a stop, and I got out and wobbled to the door of the hotel, where I heard voices that carried from the saloon. "She's dead and it's all my fault," Eleanor cried. "I shouldn't have let those people force me outside and onto that bus. We barely escaped with our lives as the water rushed out of the mine."

"It's not your fault," Andrew said, tears running down his face as he held Eleanor when I walked into the saloon. Even Mr. Wilson was crying, until he spotted me and said, "Agnes?"

Eleanor ran toward me and hugged me tight. "Oh, Agnes. I thought I had lost you for sure."

"Big Jake saved the day, but after we had freed Unique, we climbed to the top of the mountain over the mine to safety and had to climb down the other side where the sheriff showed up looking for us. It's an escape route. There was a set of stairs that went to the top of the mountain," I explained.

"Let her go, Eleanor. I want to hug her, too," Andrew said.

Eleanor wiped her tears away and did as he requested, allowing Andrew to move in for one of the warmest hugs I'd ever experienced, and I melted into him.

"What am I going to do with you, Agnes?" he said. "Why would you do something like that?"

I pulled away. "The young lady was trapped, and I did help since it took both of the men to lift that rock off her foot. The shaft was filling so fast that she hardly was able to keep her head above the water."

"That's why I love you so much, Agnes. And about setting a wedding date—how does a Valentines Day wedding sound?"

"Get married on Valentine's Day?"

"Of course, why not?"

"Sounds like a plan. How about it, Mr. Wilson?" Eleanor asked. "We could have a double wedding."

Our plans were made over dinner, and Mrs. Barry was bummed when she learned that she wouldn't be able to tour the Lemon Pine Mine after all. Mrs. Peacock tried her best to flirt with Mr. Wilson, but he never even looked at her. He spent the good part of the dinner gazing into Eleanor's eyes and kissing the back of her hand with butterfly kisses. Any other time I'd have thought *eww*, but it was just so sweet, and even Caroline smiled as she stood close by with a man in a tweed suit who was also a ghost. I figured this was Niles, but as I saw a black mist form behind them, I knew in a heartbeat that I'd meet Crazy Mary at last.

I stared at the black mist as it flew into Caroline, and they went tumbling into the table next to them, scattering the chairs and then ricocheting through the ceiling with Niles following them.

"What on Earth?" Mrs. Barry said, standing.

"Probably not really supposed to be on earth," I said. "Didn't you know that this place is haunted?"

"Well, no. Really? So that's why there was a black mist that just went into the ceiling."

"You saw that, Mrs. Barry?" Mrs. Peacock asked. "I didn't see it."

"That's because you were trying to get Mr. Wilson's attention. Knock it off already; didn't you just hear that Mr. Wilson is marrying Eleanor?"

Eleanor stretched. "It's sure getting late. I think I'll retire for the night."

"Sounds like a plan," Mr. Wilson said with a wicked grin.

Once the happy couple was out of sight, I stood, too. "I'm with them, or not *with* them. I-I'm just exhausted after my ordeal today."

As Andrew and I walked back to the elevator, The Cutter was slashing at Mr. Wilson, who was defending himself by swinging his walker at him. "Stay away from my woman, you ... you *entity*. She's mine."

"That's where you're wrong. She's mine now," The Cutter said.

"Now, boys, stop this," Eleanor said as she stomped a foot.

"Please, Douglas," I implored him. "Eleanor and Mr. Wilson are engaged and he's ... well, he's alive." The Cutter frowned and floated back into the library and we followed. "I'm sorry," I said. "Why don't you find someone like you?"

"Like me?"

"Yes. Another ghost lives in the attic all alone, too. Perhaps you should meet. Her name is Mary."

"Crazy Mary you mean, right? She's too busy chasing after that man of hers, Niles."

"I know, but have you ever actually met her, and perhaps tried to speak to her?"

"With all that stomping around she does all night, I doubt she'd even give me the time of day."

"I believe she's busy at the moment, but how about if I go up there tomorrow with you and introduce you two?"

"You've met her?"

"Well, no, but how hard can it be to introduce the two of you?"

"I'm not sure, but I'll give it a try. I hope this knife doesn't scare her."

"I'm sure that she'll understand since she's a spirit herself."

"Okay, tomorrow, then."

I led the way from the library and Andrew shook his head. "It's like you're a ghost whisperer."

"Very uncanny," Mr. Wilson added.

We went up to our respective rooms and I fell into bed. "Andrew, could you come with me tomorrow to check out Peyton Leister's cabin? It's out of town. If I can't find the family there, I promise that I'll give up the investigation."

"Okay, but only if you promise that will be the end of it."

I nodded. He took me into his arms and we fell asleep in each other's arms within minutes.

In the morning, I had to soak in a hot bath until the ache in my muscles subsided, and by the time I was downstairs for breakfast, I told Eleanor how I planned to search for Peyton Leister's cabin.

Mr. Wilson smiled and said, "I'd like to come along with you, if you don't mind."

"I'm not sure. I mean, the terrain might be too rough for your walker."

"If it is, I can wait in the Jeep."

"Okay, man," Andrew, said. "That way, if we get into any trouble, you can go for help."

GHOSTLY HIJINKS

After breakfast, we donned the proper footwear, loaded into the Jeep and were off down the road. "So where is the cabin anyway?" Andrew asked.

"Oh, I'm not sure, but in my dream I saw a cabin, so it must be off Highway 50 near where we came into town. Perhaps within a few miles, I'm thinking. Big Jake wasn't all that specific."

"Okay, so you want me to head back down Highway 50 and don't even know for sure where this cabin even is?"

"Don't try to analyze it, man," Mr. Wilson said. "Just go with it. The ghost whisperer can't be wrong."

We drove along the highway, leaving Silver behind, and I thought and thought about Caroline, but she never showed up. I then knew that it was up to me to remember what I had seen in my dream and stared at the terrain. We passed barren areas that were more desert-looking with tumbleweeds blowing in the wind.

I closed my eyes and thought hard, *Where are you*? When I opened my eyes again, I shouted, "Stop!"

Andrew halted the Jeep and I stared at a shadow cast on the ground near where we were. "I think this is the right place." Of course, in my dream it had been a spirit, not simply a shadow that had no purpose to be there.

"Are you sure?"

"Please, Andrew, I'm sure," I said as I squeezed his hand.

We got out of the Jeep, but kept the motor running with Mr. Wilson inside, playing lookout. "If you're not back in an hour, I'm calling the sheriff via this button." He pointed out the 911-call button in the Jeep.

"Of course, it can't hurt to have given the sheriff a heads up before we headed out here," Andrew said, "Which is why I called him while you were in the tub."

"Oh, and what was his response?"

"To be extra careful."

"Well, at least someone knows where we are, in case we get into trouble or trapped."

"I could do without the trapped part, Agnes," Andrew scolded me.

"Sorry, but with this investigative stuff, you just never know what will happen."

I walked the way I thought I had in my dream, except this time around, I had to climb a hill as Eleanor asked, "Are you sure this is the right direction?"

When we reached the crest of the hill and there was a cabin below in a valley of sorts, I said, "Yup."

We descended the hill that was not too steep or gravel-covered, and strode toward the stone cabin that looked quite old. "That cabin looks over a hundred years old," I said.

"How can you be sure, Agnes?" Eleanor asked.

I stared at the ground, noting footprints of varying sizes. "Someone might be here now, look," I whispered pointing out the footprints.

"We shouldn't be here," Eleanor whispered back.

"Let's just sneak over to the cabin and see if anyone's here."

We stepped carefully so as not to disturb any stones and waltzed up to the cabin, listening intently, but all I heard was the roar of the wind. I made my way for the door before I could be stopped and opened it, swinging it open. There was nobody there so I strode inside. Empty cans blanketed the floor of the cabin and I stooped to see what they were. "Some of these aren't all that old."

There was one bed with ripped bedding and a table with one chair that was tipped over. I picked up one lone strand of blonde hair from the table and raised a brow. "In my dream, Rebecca had blonde hair."

"It could be anybody," Eleanor said.

I lifted a torn rug that was in the middle of the floor and beneath it was a trap door. I lifted it, listening for movement below, but there was none. I moved to the ladder to climb down and Andrew stopped me. "I don't think that's a good idea."

"Fine, then you go down there and see where it leads, but I'm not about to stay up here when you're down there."

"Fine, I'll go down first, and then you and Eleanor can come down if the coast is clear."

"Go right ahead," Eleanor said. "I'm staying right up here."

"Suit yourself, but I hope you're intent on defending yourself if someone shows up here."

Eleanor armed herself with a piece of firewood she'd found and settled into the chair as Andrew went down first, signaling me to come down next. "We'll call if we need help, Eleanor."

Once we were all the way down, we stood on the floor of a cave, or mineshaft. "This might be where Peyton Leister found all of his gold."

Andrew shrugged. "If it was, I highly doubt someone wouldn't have been able to find his stash."

"If he hid his stash here, you mean. He very well might have hid it elsewhere, I suppose." Andrew had a valid point, but that would just be too easy.

We went down the corridor, grabbing a lighted hat that hung on the wall. Once we had the hats on and flipped on the light, we followed the tunnel until it opened up, and on one wall was a cell of some sort. I ran there, but it was empty. Except for the mummified corpse that was on a cot!

"I bet that's Peyton Leister, and someone had him imprisoned here."

"Why?"

"Well, the story goes that he was never found, and his grave was empty at the cemetery. Whoever kept him here was trying to force him to tell where he hid the gold bars is my thinking. I guess he never gave it up, which is why he's lying dead there."

On the bars was more blonde hair, which disturbed me so much. "There's more blonde hair, Andrew. Do you think someone was holding the family here?"

"For all we know, the family came here of their own accord, but I don't see them so …"

"They might be further up the tunnel, and we better hurry since we don't know what provisions they might have."

I led the way with Andrew begrudgingly following. We walked for what seemed like forever until I heard a whimper and raced ahead, but I couldn't see anything. "Keep searching," Caroline whispered in my ear, and I did what she told me to do, continuing on, but before we made it very far, I saw a child huddled on the floor, a child with blonde hair. I raced over there and asked, "Are you okay, Rebecca?"

"H-How do you know my name?" she asked, her blue eyes glowing in the light of my helmet light.

"Are you all alone here?"

"Yes, I can't find my family."

"Oh, you poor dear," I said as I hugged her tightly. When I released her, I asked, "Did you come down here with your parents?"

"Yes. A man told my parents there was gold down here, but they never found any, just worked for days looking. Yesterday when I woke up, I couldn't find my parents and I was all alone." She whimpered.

"Who brought your family down here?"

"Some man. He was nice most the time, except when my parents didn't work hard enough with their axes. Then he became very angry. He told them if they didn't work harder that they'd end up like the other family."

Andrew motioned that he was going to look further in the tunnel, but I helped Rebecca up and went back to where Andrew and I had climbed down, yelling up to Eleanor and told her to get the sheriff and quick. I then sent the little girl up the ladder since I had no idea if whoever had held Rebecca's family was still here somewhere.

I went back in search of Andrew, who met me halfway. "The tunnel ends a few hundred feet up and nobody's here."

I sighed. "Oh, no. I had so hoped that we'd find the family here."

"I wonder where else they could be?"

"Beats me, but hopefully the sheriff can figure it out."

We went back up the tunnel and waited in the cabin until Sheriff Bradley and a few other men entered the cabin. "We found the missing girl, Rebecca, but her family is still missing. I'm just afraid for their lives right now. A man brought them down here and forced them to work one of the tunnels for gold. There's a cell down there, too, with a corpse inside. I think it might be Peyton Leister. Someone was holding him here, I think, possibly to force him to tell where he hid the gold bars."

"Lead the way, please," the sheriff said.

When we were at the cell, the door opened easily and the sheriff took a look at the remains, fingering a hole in the fabric of its shirt. "Looks like he might have been shot. If this really is Peyton Leister, this is the reason they never found his body in the desert. I'll go up to the ridge and radio the anthropologist to remove the remains. He's in town to hand me his report about the body at the Goldberg Hotel."

After the body was removed, we were all in the sheriff's office as he went over his report. Rebecca had been taken to an undisclosed location until her parents were located, since the sheriff insisted that we keep our mouths shut about what we'd found in that cabin, which we agreed to since it might not be wise to tip the bad guy off if he was part of this community.

"Seems that the anthropologist said that the remains at the hotel indeed are well over one hundred years old, and the woman was indeed pregnant, but the baby died with her. It still remains inside her corpse."

"So it might not be related to Francine Pullman's family at all."

"Doesn't look like it, but it's still strange that nobody ever went into Room 109 in all these years."

"They said they don't have a key to Room 109. Strange how it opened for you," Andrew said.

"Strange indeed, but perhaps the spirit of that poor woman just wouldn't rest until she was found. Will you be checking if it might be this Elizabeth that everyone has said was involved with Jessup Goldberg?"

"The prostitute? I suppose if we can positively identify her and check the DNA of her descendants, but the descendants of Jessup's have vehemently denied that this Elizabeth was ever here at the hotel at the same time as Jessup—that he spent the majority of his time in Reno."

"That doesn't mean he never came back here, or kept her here waiting for him."

"True, but then again, it might just turn out to be one of life's little mysteries that just can't be solved."

"Which I so hope the family won't be."

We said our goodbyes and made it back to the hotel where Eleanor and Mr. Wilson awaited us. "I'm so sorry I left you to find that body down there all by yourself," Eleanor said.

"I wasn't alone. Andrew was with me, and Caroline encouraged me to keep searching for the little girl."

"No, I didn't, Agnes," Caroline said as she appeared next to me. "I've been kept too busy running from Crazy Mary all day."

"We'll talk about that another time. I'm trying to sort out where the missing family might be."

"Oh, so they still haven't been found, then?" Francine asked from behind me. "I had hoped that you had forgotten all about that."

"I have, really. I promised Andrew if I couldn't find the family today that I'd just forget about it. I'm sure the sheriff will uncover the truth eventually."

"Really? I don't see you as the quitting type."

"Well, we need to head on home soon. I have a wedding to plan."

"Oh, really? Whose?"

"Andrew and I have been engaged for quite a while and we finally set a date."

"And Mr. Wilson, and me," Eleanor added. "We're going to have a double wedding."

"How nice," Francine said stiffly. "I'm sure going to miss you girls. You've really livened up the hotel."

She walked away with a clacking of heels and I relaxed. "That woman really bugs me."

"She might rub you the wrong way, Agnes, but you can't pin any wrongdoing on her now. She never did know about the remains and her family wasn't guilty of murdering that woman."

"You're quite right, Eleanor. I'd love to pin something on her, but I'm not ready to railroad anyone, especially if they aren't guilty of a crime."

Hours later, sleep just wouldn't come, but it sure did for Andrew who was sawing all kinds of logs from the sounds of it. All I could think about was just where the family had been taken and where else in town the mysterious man might have them digging next. If they weren't able to find the gold the man was after, they might not live to see too many more days.

I turned on my side and closed my eyes, trying to drown out the sounds of Andrew's snoring when I finally gave up and got up, putting on my robe. I'd just go downstairs and raid the refrigerator; a warm glass of milk might help.

When I opened my door, Eleanor popped her head out of her door, too. "Where are you going this time of night?"

"Shhh," I said, motioning to the elevator.

Once we were inside the elevator and the door closed, I said, "I can't sleep. Was planning to raid the fridge."

"Sounds like a plan."

"That blasted ghost upstairs has kept me awake. All that pacing is driving me nuts."

"At least she quit chasing Caroline."

"That's what you think, but for the moment she's given it a rest," Caroline said as she bobbed next to me.

When we were in the kitchen, I found the milk and poured it into two cups, warming them in the microwave. "I sure wish I could have a cup," Caroline said. "The worst part of being dead is that I can't eat. What I'd do for a bowl of ice cream."

"I bet. I know that would surely do me in."

We sat in the empty dining room and I enjoyed my milk, but I was startled by a noise. I cocked my head sideways and listened again. *Thump*. I continued to listen to the thump that came about ever thirty seconds. *Thump*.

"Does anyone else hear that?" I asked.

"What are we supposed to be hearing?" asked Eleanor.

"That thumping noise. It kinda reminds me of when we were at the Lemon Pine Mine and Unique and Ramone were hammering away looking for *gold*."

We jumped up and I led the group, following the sound that only I could hear. *Thump*. I moved toward the elevator. *Thump*. When I walked into the elevator, the noise was much louder. *Thump*.

"I heard it that time, Agnes," Eleanor said. "But where could that be coming from? It sounds like it's coming from below us somewhere."

"Sound carries like that." I stared at the M button on the elevator and pushed it before anyone could stop me.

GHOSTLY HIJINKS

"Agnes, no," Eleanor said.

The elevator descended and the M button lit up and was flashing, but as the elevator continued to move downward, the thumping became much louder. *Thump! Thump! Thump!*

"I sure hope nobody knows we're coming," I said.

I held on to the bar on the side of the elevator as it picked up speed. "How deep is this mine anyway?"

"I guess we'll find out soon enough."

The elevator came to a screeching halt and the door flew open. Luckily, nobody was there, but I continued to hear the thumping as I made my way up the tunnel of what looked to be a mineshaft of some sort. After we'd walked two hundred feet, I heard a man say, "Okay, take a break. You have five minutes."

"Is that all? Please let us go, we won't tell anyone. We promise."

"I'll let you go when you find what I'm looking for."

"I miss my daughter. Please, you left her all alone back in the other place and we didn't find anything there, either. She needs me," the woman implored the man.

"She'll be fine. I left plenty of water."

"But she's only five."

"Two more minutes, then you're back to work and you better hope you find something this time or the buzzards will be plucking your carcasses clean come morning."

"But we've done all you've asked."

"No, you haven't. You've yet to find the gold."

Why does that voice sound so familiar? My thoughts were interrupted as another man said, "Have you ever considered that there's no gold down here?"

"Yes, they told us at the Willington General Store that the mineshaft was built down here, but no gold was ever found," the woman said.

"Time's up. Get back to work. You only have a few hours left before it won't be safe to be making this much racket."

"We should go for help," Eleanor whispered in my ear.

"There's no time," I whispered back. "From the sounds of it, this family doesn't have much time left." I walked forward and into the light where the family was now pounding away at the wall, facing down the source of their anxiety—Redd Bullet—the jack-of-all-trades for the Goldberg Hotel & Saloon!

Chapter Fifteen

Redd panned his head sideways, his eyes widening considerably. "Wh-What are you doing down here?" he asked, pulling a gun from his pants, pointing it at me.

"Put that gun down, Redd," I said. "What are you doing? Let those people go."

"Why did you have to come down here? I thought you had given up on the missing family."

"Given up is not part of who I am. We've found Rebecca and she's safely tucked away," I told the couple. "I assume you're Trisha and Aaron Jameson, right?"

"Who are you?" Trisha asked, nodding with tears in her eyes.

"I'm Agnes Barton and I'm here to help you folks like I helped your daughter."

"You're not going to help anyone. You're as good as dead."

"Where's the love, Redd?" I asked. "I must admit that I'm really shocked that you're here. You do know you won't find Leister's gold down here, right?"

"I figured that when I didn't find it in the last place, I had to search somewhere else."

"Except that you know there's no gold here, so why torment this couple?"

"Leister's gold is somewhere in Silver and this is as good a place as any. Nobody knows for sure when he actually came to Silver, or where he hid his gold. I'm thinking that this would be the last place anyone would ever look."

179

"Except that Jessup dug the mine down here. So unless Peyton came to Silver after the hotel was built, Leister's gold isn't down here."

"Would you just shut up? I'm trying to think."

"Is Francine in with you on this? I wouldn't be surprised, really."

"That cow? I think not. I knew who she was when I met her in Phoenix that night when I came to her room to fix the plumbing, and that was all planned."

"So you wanted a woman with money? Except that according to her, you were never romantically involved."

"Nope, but I knew the story about Leister's gold and planned to find it when I came here."

"Except you never found it. So why stay all these years?"

"I'll find it someday, and when I do, I'll disappear just like so many of the families have. The thing is that they only know about two of them when it's been closer to five. If only that damn Lois hadn't started blabbing about the missing family."

"Actually, I believe divine intervention is involved this time since I dreamed about this family, or Rebecca. I have a few gifts, like being able to see ghosts, and now I dream about things that are really happening or about to happen—like Rebecca being separated from her family. I even dreamed about the actor, Sheriff Wilford, and Francine, even the way the hotel looked although I'd never been here before."

"You really need your head checked. Sure, ghosts exist here, but they can't hurt anybody."

I laughed. "I wouldn't say that too loud, The Cutter might hear you!" I shouted loud enough to hope that he'd appear.

"Good try, but he never leaves the library and you already know that."

I moved aside as The Cutter raced forward with all the might of a steam engine, swinging that jagged blade of his. Trisha and Aaron ran toward me and we huddled together as Redd emptied his gun at The Cutter, who only smirked with a disembodied laugh as the bullets went right through him and whizzed dangerously close to us. We raced up the tunnel and toward the elevator as Redd sprinted after us. "Get back here," Redd shouted.

Right before he caught up with us, Redd was besieged by spirits who pushed him back, The Cutter swinging his jagged blade at him, nicking Redd's skin, and he shrieked as he raced away, screaming. Within minutes, I heard a high-pitched scream I had to check out, sending the others back to the elevator.

Eleanor came out from where she was hiding. "No way am I leaving you alone again," Eleanor said as she accompanied me.

I followed the screams and found that Redd had fallen through where the wall had given way and he held the ledge, frantically shouting, "Help me!"

"How on earth do you think we can pull you up?"

"I-I'm slipping."

"You better hold on while we go for help," I said, knowing that we'd never be able to pull him up without him yanking us in with him.

By the time we made it back with help in the form of Sheriff Bradley and a few other burly men, Redd had lost his grip and had fallen to his death twenty feet below, atop a pile of gold bars!

"Well, it looks like Redd finally found his gold," I said.

"Except that he's not around to reap the benefits," Eleanor added.

"At least the missing family was found and not murdered. I assume he murdered the Thompsons," the sheriff said.

"Yes, he told us he murdered five families. He's been forcing them to find Leister's gold for him, and when they didn't find it, he got rid of them. It's sickening when I think about it. He left poor Rebecca to die. He told us that he left water for her, but I didn't see any water when we were in the tunnel under that cabin."

"Why was there a cell down there anyway?" Eleanor asked.

"Because that wasn't Peyton Leister's cabin. That was the old jailhouse at one time."

"Oh, that sure makes sense. I still can't believe that Redd stayed all these years looking for the gold, but it's good that it's finally found."

"After we retrieve Redd's body, we're going to retrieve the gold, and since it's under the Goldberg it belongs to Francine Pullman," the sheriff explained.

"The other tourists will really be disappointed that they weren't the ones to finally find it." I said.

"And most of the town, no doubt," Francine said as she joined us. "Are you ladies, okay?"

"Yes, and I'm very sorry for thinking that you were in on this with Redd, but what I don't understand is, how did that gold get into this mineshaft? I figured Peyton Leister would have been in Silver way before this hotel was ever built."

"Well, that's a different shaft—not the one Jessup dug—and a part of the Winfield Hotel that burned to the ground around 1860. Jessup had no clue just how close he was."

"What do you plan to do with the gold?"

"I'll have it equally divided so that all of the residents of Silver get their share. Besides, I'm not hurting for money. My great-grandfather started the Wisteria Hotel chain in his sober years, which I inherited and sold just recently."

"Wow, no wonder your great-grandfather never bothered to open this hotel during his lifetime, and that's sure generous of you, sharing the gold with the residents of Silver."

"It's the least I can do. We're a tight-knit group here and now the town will get a facelift it desperately needs. I also think building a small museum is in order, depicting the legend of Peyton Leister."

"I'm really sorry for thinking that your family might have been responsible for the murder of the woman in Room 109. It's my understanding that you don't have a key to open that door."

"Exactly, but I guess it's hard to understand why I'd never just break through the door, but with the amount of spirits in this place, I didn't want to press my luck."

"True, but I guess the spirit of whoever was murdered in that room wanted to rest at last. That door opened right up for us. I've been seeing ghosts since I had a car accident."

"That's quite a gift to have."

"I suppose." I didn't want to tell her how I'd planned to try to fix Crazy Mary up with The Cutter, who I had to thank for saving our life.

"What if she doesn't like me?" The Cutter asked me.

I continued to walk up the attic steps. "Have faith, man. If I didn't think you stood a chance, I'd never have brought you up here. She's lonely and pining over a ghost that doesn't want anything to do with her. What other options does she have?"

We crossed the attic floor and a woman strode forward. "Why are you here?"

"Douglas, this is Mary," I introduced them.

Mary's grotesque shape changed from monster to that of a small woman with innocent eyes. "Oh, my. I've always wanted to meet you, Mr. Cutter. I really like your style, scaring folks out of the library."

"I don't do that anymore. Agnes here was kind enough to bring me more current books to read. I'm reading Louis L'Amour right now. He writes westerns."

"I enjoy reading, too. Have you ever heard of *Fifty Shades of Grey*?"

"Is it true that you killed Niles?" I asked curiously, *so* wanting to change the subject.

"You're not supposed to ask spirits things like that," Douglas chastised me. "It's hard to remember what you did or didn't do when you're alive and it really doesn't matter, anyway."

I slunk away and left the two ghosts to get better acquainted and met Caroline on the first floor. She stood hovering as Andrew was checking us out. The sheriff told us that they have yet to be able to identify the remains in Room 109, and might never, but the remains in the old jailhouse were much easier as Peyton's Leister's journal was found with his body.

"Did you tell Niles goodbye, Caroline?" Her eyes widened and she winked at Eleanor who chuckled, but didn't say a word.

"Is there something that I don't know about? Like a secret you're keeping from me?" I asked Eleanor.

"Why would you even think that? You know Caroline and I don't even get along."

I knew better, much better than that, but I decided to let it go. Even though Caroline told Niles to remain out of sight, I knew he would be coming home with us. I could feel his presence, but if it would make Caroline happy, who was I to tell her that she couldn't bring him home with us. I only hoped that he wouldn't cause too many problems at the Butler Mansion.

As we drove out of Silver, I really was happy to be heading back home. Trips are nice, but I hadn't been prepared to stay in a real haunted hotel and hoped that Redd's ghost wouldn't be roaming the place now. When the sheriff searched his room, he found bags filled with gold nuggets and dust. So it seemed that all the gold isn't gone from Silver quite yet. Instead of keeping any of it as a reward offered by Francine for all we'd done to solve the mystery, I gave it to the Jameson family, who were staying in Silver and given jobs at the Goldberg Hotel.

As for Silver, it will remain as timeless as ever and a real ghost town in more ways than one, containing more secrets than most will ever know, which is really how it should be. It remains a favorite tourist stop on Highway 50. If you can find it, that is.

Disclaimer

Silver, Nevada, is a figment of the author's imagination.

About the Author

USA Today Bestseller Madison Johns isn't the type of writer who publishes one book a year. She works hard to publish once a month, whether it's one of her beloved Agnes Barton mysteries, or paranormal romances. Watching established authors, she realized early on that it's not good to keep readers waiting for her next book too long. She prefers to burn the midnight oil with a strict publishing schedule, meeting her deadlines at any cost. Animal-lover Madison lives in mid-Michigan with her two children and animals galore, including a hilarious Jackson Chameleon.

Visit her on the web at: http://madisonjohns.com where you'll find a form to sign up for her mystery and paranormal romance newsletters.

Other Books By Madison Johns

<u>An Agnes Barton Senior Sleuth Mystery Series</u>

Armed and Outrageous

Grannies, Guns & Ghosts

Senior Snoops

Trouble in Tawas

Treasure in Tawas

Bigfoot in Tawas

<u>Agnes Barton Paranormal Mystery</u>

Haunted Hijinks

<u>Kimberly Steele Romance Novella (Sweet Romance)</u>

Pretty and Pregnant

<u>An Agnes Barton/Kimberly Steele Cozy Mystery</u>

Pretty, Hip & Dead

<u>A Cajun Cooking Mystery</u>

Target of Death

<u>Kelly Gray (Stand alone) Sweet Romance</u>

Redneck Romance

<u>Paranormal Romance</u>

Hidden, Clan of the Werebear (Part One)

Discovered, Clan of the Werebear (Part Two)

Betrayed, Clan of the Werebear (Part Three)

Katlyn: Shadow Creek Shifters

(Red-hot ménage shifter romance-Book One)